# NOTHING BUT A DARE

MOLLY O'HARE

Cover art: Wildelake Creative
Photographer: Furiousfotog: Golden Czermak
Model: Michael J Scanlon

**Disclaimer:** This title is intended for mature audiences due to adult situations and languages.

Molly O'Hare

First Print: Sept 2019

Be You Publishing, LLC

www.MollyOHareauthor.com

# ACKNOWLEDGMENTS

Thank you! Yes, you. From the bottom of my heart, I appreciate every single reader out there. Not just my readers, but all readers. Thank you for exploring new worlds, falling in love multiple times, slaying dragons, and riding them. But what is a storyteller, if we have no one to tell the story to?

Oh man, this is tough. There are so many people I want to thank. I think with each book this list gets longer and longer. From my ride or die, Richelle (she's the one that pushes me to publish. If it weren't for her, none of these books would be here) to my author friends and reader group. I do not know what I would be without any of you. I could list probably a million names here.

My sprint group: Holy effe me. If it weren't for you all this book wouldn't have gotten done. Allysa, Rayanna, Maren, Lesley, everyone. You all kept me on track and I'm forever grateful.

Angela Verdenius, you are one of my best friends. It still blows my mind how you took me under your wing as a writer when I was only a faithful reader of yours. I am so grateful for you!

Jody Kaye, girl, thank you for always checking in on me, sending me positive mindset and always believing I can do anything I put my mind to. You are a gem.

Cassie-Ann who knew a kick ass friendship would form after one commonality between us. Thank you for always, freaking always believing in me. You are sent from the Universe and I am beyond grateful.

My RomCom groups. Well, shit where do I even start? From my RomCom Authors Network, to RomCom Junkies. All of you are amazing. I wouldn't be here without you. Laura, Sylvie, Marika, Heather, Brenda, Elizabeth, Julia, Ceri, KL, Stephanie, Susannah, Jami, Cassie-Ann, Nikky all of you. You are so freaking amazing.

My Reader Group, who've become like family to me. Gail, Amy, Rubi, Elizabeth, Jennifer, Kelly, Charlene, Chantal, Jenn. Oh, god I can name a crap ton more. You all mean so freaking much to me. You'll never understand it.

To everyone that helped make this book possible, from cover art, editing, photography, proofreading, everything. There is so much that goes into publishing a story and I'm so thankful for the group I get to work alongside with. Every one of them means something to me. Golden, Michael, Karen, Richelle, you all mean so much to me.

There are so many more people I want to thank, but the announcer is about to shut off my mic. Just know I am so fucking grateful from the bottom of my heart for every single one of you.

# DEDICATION

*I dedicate this story to you and to anyone who has ever felt less. Remember you are unique, you are special. Try not to forget other people's opinions of you, are none of your concern. It only matters what you think of you.*
*You live your whole life with only one body, one mind, one soul. There is no one in this world that is exactly like you, and that's a miracle.*
*You're a motherfucking unicorn.*
*Own that shit!*

# CHAPTER ONE

"I DARE YOU."

Hunter James raised his brow at ten-year-old Abbie Collins as she braced herself on the highest tree branch in their neighboring backyards. She quickly moved her eyes from him to reassess her surroundings. From where Abbie balanced, things weren't looking too good. How in the world had she gotten herself into this mess?

*And again...*

Her eyes moved back to the boy taunting her.

Oh yeah, how could she forget?

Hunter freaking James.

He's the reason she was now in a tree.

Since Hunter moved in next door with his dad and stepmom, he was constantly causing trouble. And somehow, Abbie was always involved.

She closed her eyes as she held onto the tree trunk tightly.

The day Hunter and his family moved in, Abbie and her mother, Kathleen, brought them over fresh baked cookies. That was the nice thing to do, after all. The neighborly thing.

Plus, Abbie had been particularly proud of this batch since she spent hours decorating each one with the word 'welcome'.

Abbie, along with her mother, had considered herself the welcoming committee of the neighborhood.

Ehh, what could she say? She got her nurturing side from her mom. Plus, Abbie absolutely adored making new friends. You could *never* have too many if you asked her.

The more, the merrier.

Maybe it was because Abbie didn't have any brothers or sisters, or maybe it was her need for everyone to feel like they belonged.

After her father abandoned her and her mom right after Abbie was born there was always something lacking. That could've been the reason why her mother always made it a point to welcome anyone that moved in with wide open arms and a plate full of cookies. She needed them to feel wanted since they'd never felt that.

Well, that plate full of cookies was two years ago and every day since meeting Hunter James, Abbie regretted every freaking second of it.

"Are you gonna do it or what?" Hunter taunted from below. "You better hurry, I don't know if that branch will hold you much longer?"

*Jerk.* Abbie's eyes narrowed at him as she held onto the tree trunk a little tighter. If she could go back in time, she would have added salt to the cookies, or better yet, maybe some arsenic.

"Stop being a baby, Collins."

"I'm not being a baby!" Abbie felt the branch bend under her weight.

Quickly, she closed her eyes as her heart started to pound against her chest. Okay, so she knew she was only about six feet off the ground, and the likelihood of her causing severe damage was slim to none; however, the more she looked at the annoying boy below her, the farther away he seemed.

Abbie took a deep breath before she opened her eyes and looked back at Hunter.

That's when she noticed it.

Hunter was staring at her with that stupid smug smirk on his face. The same one he always got when he thought he'd won.

A growl erupted from deep inside her. *Not today!*

If Abbie were on the ground and *not* a million feet in the air, she'd march right up to him and smack that dang smirk right off his stupid face.

Stupid Hunter.

Stupid tree.

Stupid dare!

For two years now, Hunter James had made her life a living hell.

If he wasn't constantly picking on her, he was daring her to do something she didn't want to do.

And *that* was the exact reason she was up in a tree right now.

*"You're too scared, Abbie." Hunter laughed as he crossed his arms over his chest.*

*"Am not. I just think it's dumb to jump out of a tree unless there is a logical reason to do so."*

*"Why do you always do that?" He glared at her.*

*"Do what?"*

*"Say shit to make you sound all smart and stuff."*

*"I am* smart, *unlike you dumb-dumb."*

*Hunter's eyes narrowed before his lips formed into that smirk. "I dare you."*

A Collins never surrendered.

A Collins never backed down.

A Collins never turned down a dare.

At least that's what her mother would say. Okay, not so much the dare part, but the never backing down part. Collins' were strong, and no matter what was thrown at them, they always ended up on top.

*No one will ever knock us down.*

Not her deadbeat father, and certainly not Hunter James.

And that left Abbie here.

About to jump to her death.

She rolled her eyes at herself. *Maybe death was a little dramatic.* She took another deep breath before looking at the ground. Her breath caught in her throat as Hunter suddenly seemed very far away. *Actually, death could be a possibility.*

"You scared?" Hunter shouted.

"Not as scared as you were when I dared you to jump off the roof into the pool," she snapped.

"I did it, didn't I?"

"Only after I called you a chicken," she yelled back. Why couldn't she have just walked away? Any other normal human being would have, but no. Abbie was now two years deep in some messed up back and forth dare-off.

"And that's what you're being right now. Abbie the chicken!" The corner of his mouth turned up into that stupid smirk again. "That's your new name."

"When I get down there, I'm gonna hit you!"

"You'd have to catch me first."

Abbie's eyes narrowed in on her target. She hated him. With every ounce of her being, she hated Hunter James.

*Screw it.*

She jumped.

Thankfully something broke her fall.

That something being Hunter James.

"What the hell?" Hunter cried. "You weren't supposed to jump on me, Collins."

"You never specified what I had to do in the dare. If you wanted to make sure I *didn't* jump on you, then you needed to disclose those terms upfront." She huffed as she righted herself making it so she sat on Hunter's chest. She then pushed her chestnut hair out of her face. "It's not my fault your dumb brain forgot that part."

"Who talks like that?" He squirmed trying to get her off. "Has anyone ever told you, you're annoying?"

"Yes, you. Every day."

"You're ten. You're not some genius." Hunter pushed her off him, causing her to land on her butt in the dirt.

From where she landed, Abbie watched as he fixed his clothes before pushing his black hair out of his face, giving her the view of his hunter green eyes that matched his name. "Excuse you, I turn eleven in two days." Abbie stuck her tongue out at him as she jumped to her feet.

"Oh, that reminds me..." Hunter pulled a tiny box out of his pocket. "This is for you."

Abbie took a step back caught entirely off-guard. Then out of nowhere, her heart did this weird flip thing she couldn't explain.

As she stared at him, with her mouth open in disbelief. She quickly tried to scan her body. She was ten, so there was no way she was having a heart attack. Right? When Hunter pushed the box closer to her, her heart did it again.

*What the hell? Am I dying? Oh, God, the jump really did kill me. And, of course, this is now my hell. A hell where Hunter James existed.*

"Take the box, Abbie," Hunter scoffed annoyed.

Had he really gotten her a birthday gift? She looked at the box and then back to his face. He *seemed* sincere. But then again, this was Hunter after all.

Abbie bit her bottom lip as she took the box. *Maybe this is the end of the feud...or, you know, maybe it was a bomb.* There was a fifty-fifty shot of either one.

*Screw it.* That was Abbie's motto when it came to Hunter.

She opened the box.

"Eww!" Before Abbie knew what was happening, grasshoppers started jumping out causing her to drop the box.

"Happy Birthday!" Hunter laughed as Abbie danced around trying to get the creatures off. "You're a jerk, Hunter."

"No, I'm not." He took a step closer to her plucking one of the grasshoppers off her shoulder. "I dare you to eat it."

"No way!" Abbie shook her head stepping back from him.

"You scared, little girl?" He pushed the grasshopper closer to her face.

"No, I'm not scared."

"Abbie the chicken. I knew the name would fit."

*Screw it!*

Abbie snatched the grasshopper from Hunter's fingers before shoving the thing into her mouth causing Hunter's eyes to widen for a split second before his amusement overtook him. "Holy crap. I can't believe you did it."

"Of course, I did," she said disgusted with herself. "I'm *not* a chicken."

"Abbie Babbie, the one with too much flabby," Hunter laughed.

"That's it." Abbie launched herself at Hunter tackling him to the ground. "What's your problem?"

"I don't have a problem. *You* have a problem." He fought from under her.

"Oh, that's really mature." Abbie kept him pinned to the ground. She'd learned a few things from their past wrestling matches. Like how locking her knees around his chest would prevent him from moving for at least a few seconds.

"I *am* a mature person. I'm almost thirteen. That makes me almost a teenager." Hunter looked at her. The moment her eyes locked with his green ones, that strange feeling in her heart came back. Maybe she *was* having a heart attack.

"You're a jerk."

"You always say that."

"That's 'cause it's true."

Hunter grunted before pushing Abbie off him effectively flipping her onto the ground. "Whatever. Why don't you run on home and stick your head in one of those stupid books you always have with you?"

"How is that an insult?" Abbie crossed her arms over her chest. "You make it seem like reading is a *bad* thing. Maybe if you picked up a book every once in a while, you'd actually learn something."

"Oh, like the books *you* read teach you anything?" He cocked his brow.

"Duhh. They teach me all kinds of stuff." Abbie walked to her bag and threw one of her books at him. "I dare you."

Hunter caught it with ease. "You dare me to what?"

"Read a book. Learn something. Stop being such an ass-hat."

Ignoring her new insult, Hunter cocked his head to the side. "You want me to read *Treasure Island?* This isn't English class, Collins."

"What are you scared you might actually learn something?"

Abbie knew she had him. Hunter *never* turned down a dare from her. Just like she never turned down a dare from him. "I *dare* you to read that whole book, Hunter."

His eyes shot to hers as they narrowed. "Fine." He placed the book under his arm as he turned away from her. After walking a few steps, he looked over his shoulder. "A dare's a dare. Just remember this isn't over."

*Would it ever be?*

# CHAPTER TWO

## SIXTEEN YEARS LATER

*Son of a bitch!*

Abbie tripped as she ran down the corridor towards the elevator. Of all the days to have her alarm not go off, today was *not* the day.

Not when she was ten minutes from leading the biggest meeting of her career.

Abbie clutched her bag closer to her side as she glanced at her watch. *Shit!* Maybe if she sprinted up the twenty-six flights of stairs, she'd get there with a few minutes to spare?

As soon as the thought entered her head, it left. She rolled her eyes so hard she almost gave herself a migraine.

Who the hell was she kidding?

She'd make it up one set of stairs before she'd be huffing and puffing. By the third set, she'd probably pass out. Plus, who in the hell takes the stairs? It would be six months before someone found her.

Elevator it was.

When Abbie rounded the last corner in the hall, she saw her prize. She watched as a sales representative which she believed worked on the tenth floor enter the elevator.

She looked down at her watch again.

*Fuck it.*

Modesty completely thrown out the window Abbie propelled herself to a full-on sprint towards her target.

Well, as best of a sprint she could do. Running had never been her strong suit. The only marathons she did were binge-watching shows or marathon reading.

Shoes to ground, not so much.

And right now, Abbie didn't give a rat's ass how she looked running down through the lobby. Not when the most sought-after client was upstairs waiting for her presentation. If she signed Robert Jefferson, it would go down as one of the biggest accounts in advertising history. That's all that mattered.

Landing the hard to please, CEO of Jefferson Exports was far more important than the fact her breasts were now bouncing at such a velocity, they were seconds from giving her a black eye. Plus, the sounds of her extra lumps and bumps had now become her soundtrack.

It was like she was Rocky. And her body noises were now her theme song.

Abbie watched as the guy who'd gotten onto the elevator finally noticed her. His face held a mix of terror and disbelief.

*Get ready, dude, 'cause I'm not stopping.* The moment she saw his hand move toward the elevator buttons she glared at him. *I will murder you!* If she were coordinated enough to shout at him *and* run, she would have.

However, with the way her morning went. She wasn't going to chance it.

Abbie picked up her pace as the guy forcefully hit the button. When the doors started to close and with all the strength of a tiger ready to pounce, she leaped into the air, her arm stopping the elevator door just in time.

Rocky would have been proud.

When the door opened Abbie calmly walked in before shooting an evil look at the man eyeing her like she was a rabid animal. "Asshole."

"Who you calling an asshole?" He looked her up and down.

"You."

Any other time she would have chewed him out, but right now she had more important things to do.

Thank God she'd decided to wear flats today, rather than heels. Not that she ever wore heels to begin with, but on days like today, she always tried to put in that extra effort.

As she took a calming breath, ignoring the man next to her, Abbie finally saw her reflection in the elevator doors.

Her hand flew to her chest as the image startled her.

*Oh, for fuck's sake.* No wonder the guy next to her was terrified. Her hair looked like she'd put her finger in a light socket. Her black pencil skirt was hiked up to the middle of her thighs and her once white blouse was now pretty much see-through since she spilled her water on it as she ran, showing to all that looked her purple polka dot bra with her breasts spilling out.

Abbie looked to the ceiling. *Universe? What. The. Fuck?*

Doing her best Abbie pulled back the white blouse and did the whole it's too hot movement trying to dry out her shirt. She shimmied down her pencil skirt and ran her fingers through her hair the best she could.

*This is as good as its gonna get.*

She shook her head as she opened up her bag and pulled out her presentation notes. As she scanned through them she saw the chewed corner, she couldn't help but chuckle.

Leave it to Rupert to take claim of everything as his. It was like his own little way for Abbie to remember him when she wasn't home.

Her hairless Sphynx cat never ceased to amaze her.

Moving her eyes back to her notes Abbie felt her confidence grow. It might have been a shitty morning, but she knew she had this. She'd worked hard the last two and a half months putting together something Robert Jefferson would be a fool to turn down.

Plus, Abbie knew if she could get Mr. Jefferson to sign on with William Clark Michaels Advertising, that promotion to Account Executive was hers. She could taste it. Sure, her Creative Director role was great and all, but she wanted more. She wanted a challenge.

And she'd earned it.

When the elevator chimed, she threw her notes back into her bag and did her best to pat down her hair as she headed toward the conference room.

With her shoulders back and her head held high, she walked through the door.

She froze.

As in full-on, she was ninety-nine percent sure her heart just stopped.

Right in front of her sat her boss and owner of WCM Advertising, Bill Michaels. To his left was their perspective client Robert Jefferson. But that wasn't what caused her sudden lack of motor skills.

Nope.

The other seat was filled with none other than Hunter James.

Hunter fucking James.

She closed her eyes tightly praying she was mistaken. Then she opened them slowly... *Fuck me!*

She would have recognized him anywhere. That deep hunter green of his eyes haunted her dreams.

As Abbie tried her best to get her heart to start again and remember how someone actually breathed, she took him in.

He'd filled out. Hunter had chiseled features and tan skin that only made his eyes pop that much more. His dark hair had that, I just rolled out of bed look, but it was also perfectly sculpted that way look. His tailored suit that almost hid his muscular arms made him look like he was actually here to shoot some pictures for the cover of some fashion magazine.

*What the fuck? Of course, he would look like this. Universe, add insult to injury, why don't cha?*

"Abbie," her boss, Bill, broke through her thoughts making her shoot her eyes to him. It wasn't missed, he was sending her a disapproving stare at her appearance.

*Great.*

Abbie looked down at her shirt once more to see her purple polka dot bra making itself known again. Seriously, it was like she had a flashing sign over her head saying look at my tits.

She quickly pulled away her shirt from her skin trying her best not to freak the fuck out.

When Bill cleared his throat, it caused her to snap her attention back to him. "Mr. Jefferson here is eager to get started, Abbie."

She nodded, still trying to figure out what warp hole she went through that brought her here.

"If you had gotten here on time," he continued. "I would have been able to make this introduction beforehand." Bill motioned toward Hunter, Abbie's eyes followed. The second Hunter came into view she was once again taken aback as she worked her mind trying to piece together what the fuck was going on.

"I want to introduce you to your new partner on the project. This is Hunter James. Mr. James comes highly sought after. I've been trying to snag him for years. As I'm sure you know, he's one of the top, if not the top Account Executives on the east coast."

*No. No fucking way!* Abbie scanned the room. This was one hundred percent some alternate universe she had walked into. Maybe if she took a step back the way she came, everything would right itself.

As she put one foot behind her to leave, Bill cocked his brow before giving her "the look."

*Shit.* Abbie cleared her throat. "I apologize, sir. I did not know Mr. James was in this field." She turned toward Hunter. "I guess he really isn't at the top. If he was, I would have known about him." Abbie shrugged, doing her best not to lose her shit.

*Where the hell was the exit to get the hell off this crazy train?*

Bill let out a deep laugh as he clasped Mr. Jefferson's shoulder. "She's a joker. I told you she was a spitfire."

Abbie's eye started to twitch as her fist clenched.

"The moment I informed Robert that *the* Hunter James was joining our firm on a trial basis he insisted on him being put on the project. I guess they've worked together in the past for a fundraiser," Bill continued.

*Are. You. Fucking. Kidding. Me?* "It would have been nice to let me know *before* this morning," she mumbled.

"It's nice to see you again, Abbie," A deep voice interrupted her boss from saying anything.

Abbie's eyes shot to Hunter. When she saw that fucking smirk appear on his face as his eyes danced with amusement; it took everything inside of her not to leap over the table and tackle him.

If they were kids, she would have done it in a heartbeat.

*I'll kill him! Before this meeting is over, I'm gonna be hauled out of here in fucking handcuffs.*

"Yes, Miss Collins," Mr. Jefferson got her attention distracting her from plotting the death of the man next to him. "I hope you don't mind. I know you've been working on this proposal for quite some time now, but when Bill here let it slip last week he was trying to recruit Hunter I had to have him on this. As you know, my company is one of the largest manufacturers and exporters of building materials. I only hire the best. That's what's kept me on top for nearly forty years. And I plan on forty more before I hand my company down to my son. I'm told WCM is the best in the business. Here is the deal, Miss Collins, things happen on my terms. I want to sign on that dotted line. I want to take this worry off my shoulders and focus on more important things. However, I don't think that will happen unless Mr. James is on this project."

Abbie forced a smile on her face. But inside her world was crashing around her. This couldn't be happening. There was no way in hell this was really going on. She tried wrapping her head around the fact that Hunter James was not only in her same career field but was less than five feet from her.

She'd never thought she'd see Hunter again.

And she was thankful for that.

Closing her eyes, Abbie was thrown back to the memory that she'd tried so hard to bury all those years ago.

The exact moment that broke who she once was.

*"Abs, I don't get it. You're such a prude," Hunter joked as he poked her shoulder. "You never have any fun."*

*"I have fun all the time."*

*"No, you don't, the only fun you have is when I force you to have fun."*

*"You don't force me to do anything." Abbie pushed at his shoulder. She enjoyed these types of interactions with Hunter.*

*The safe ones.*

*Ones where they weren't at each other's throats. Somehow over the years with their constant dare-off, they became friends or at least Abbie liked to think so. Sure, there were moments she still wanted to destroy him, but most of the time, she'd just roll her eyes, do the dare and try and find an even worse dare for him.*

*Did she want to punch his lights out still? Yeah. But, when they were in the middle of this dare-off game, something felt right.*

*No matter what was going on in the world, she knew she could count on Hunter to distract her. And he was right. If he didn't dare her to do half of the things he did, she would have kept her head in a book and never experience any excitement.*

*The adrenaline rush of who could dare the other to do something crazier was addictive.*

*Hunter* was *addictive.*

*She loved it. She loved the whole game.*

*She would never admit it, but she did.*

*To her, Hunter had become her best friend.*

*She'd take that to the grave.*

*If word got around that the school nerd, actually liked the jock and that their constant feuding was nothing more than a game, she'd be ruined. She worked hard on keeping up appearances of her hatred toward Hunter.*

*As they sat on the brick wall outside of the school auditorium, Hunter turned toward her. "Are you going to prom?" he asked.*

*"No. I'd rather gouge out my eyes with a rusty spoon than go." Abbie shuddered in disgust. "I don't need to see horny teenagers grinding up against each other. No, thank you."*

*"You're a stick in the mud."*

*Abbie rolled her eyes.* Jerk. *"Are you going?" she asked.*

*"No. I was gonna go, but something came up." He looked away from her.*

*"Oh, and what was that?" she asked. "Your stepmom finally ground you for the shitty grades you're getting? Or wait, maybe you've decided to join the traveling circus and the train leaves tomorrow?"*

*A strange look ran across Hunter's face right before he laughed. That deep laugh that always made her stomach do that stupid flip thing she hated. "That's it, Abs. I leave on the train tomorrow."*

*"I knew it." Abbie hugged her arms around her body.*

*She did think it was odd Hunter had found her sitting here and decided to join her. Their conversations were normally left to the backyard. Nonetheless, she shrugged it off.*

*School had ended hours ago. She had only stayed behind working on an English project and she imagined Hunter was there for some athletic thing.*

*Hunter broke the silence first. "Remember that time I dared you to eat a grasshopper and you did it?" he laughed.*

*Abbie shuddered in disgust. "Yeah. Don't remind me. You're such an asshole."*

*"You never do turn down a dare. Do you?" He stared her in the eyes.*

*"No and neither do you." She smiled, but something felt weird about this moment. Then again, whenever she and Hunter were together, it was always a cluster fuck of weirdness.*

*At least it was consistent.*

*"Abbie?"*

*"Yeah?" She pulled out her phone to see if her mom had sent her a text, but Hunter placed his hand over the screen causing her to look at him.*

*"I dare you," he whispered.*

*"You dare me to what?"*

*"Kiss me."*

*Abbie's eyes widened as she stared at him like he'd grown two heads. "You can't be serious, Hunter. Stop messing around."*

*"You know I am. When have I ever joked about a dare? Those are sacred. And," he stated matter-of-factly. "If I have my numbers correct. You're down by two."*

*That bastard! "I am not!" she protested. She quickly calculated the number of dares in her head from the sick game they started years ago.*

*"Yeah, you are. You* pretended *to break into the school library and repaint the mascot mural, but we both know you didn't."*

*"I did too, I just didn't break-in. I did it during school hours."*

*"Doesn't count."*

*"Whatever." She narrowed her eyes at him. It should count. She almost got caught... twice.*

*"Kiss me."*

*Abbie gave him the once over.*

*He couldn't be serious. And more importantly, why was she even thinking about it? This had to be on her top ten stupidest things list. Which not surprisingly all involved Hunter in some way shape or form.*

*Then again as Abbie looked at him, her eyes glanced to his mouth. She'd be lying if she said she hadn't thought about his lips on hers over the years. Late at night, Hunter would pop into her head during the most inopportune moments. She did her best to push them away, but there were times she indulged in her sick and twisted fantasy.*

*"If I kiss you will we be back to even?" she did her best to sound as calculated as possible. If Hunter even got a whiff of what she was really thinking, he'd use it against her.*

*As Hunter looked at her, she contemplated the strange expression on his face.*

*"Yeah, we will," he finally said after a few seconds.*

*"Fine." She leaned forward ready to kiss his cheek, but Hunter was fast. He moved his head at the last second.*

*Her lips connected with his.*

*All of a sudden that weird feeling came back in the pit of her stomach. But this time it was like an explosion.*

*Her heart raced as he deepened the kiss. She couldn't blame her increased heart rate on a heart attack. Oh, no. She knew this was one hundred percent Hunter James induced.*

*Abbie had heard horror stories about first kisses, but as far as this one went, she was mesmerized.*

*This was unlike anything she'd ever experienced before.*

*She felt Hunter's hand squeeze her hip pulling her closer to him.*

*"Dude, eww! Are you really kissing the Collins chick?" A voice interrupted them causing Hunter to jump back from her in shock.*

*Abbie's eyes shot open as she tried to figure out what had just happened.*

*"Dude, you are!" Troy yelled in amusement.*

*Hunter jumped up from where he was sitting and looked at his friend before looking back at Abbie. There was a sadness in his eyes that she couldn't quite register.*

*"Nah, man." Hunter looked back at Troy.*

*"I saw you."*

*"What can I say?" Hunter shrugged. "I wanted to see if Abbie flabby was easy." Hunter turned toward her with the godawful smirk on his face. The one she hated to admit she'd grown to love over the years. "Turns out she is."*

*Abbie sat there in shock as Hunter's teammate roared with laughter. Hunter looked at her dead in the eyes as he spoke his next words. "If you hadn't come over here I probably would have gotten into her pants. You know the bigger girls will always do whatever it takes to feel wanted."*

*Her heart stopped as her brain worked overtime trying to understand. She was in such shock she couldn't even defend herself. It was like a straight punch to the gut.*

*"Turns out she's nothing but a loser." Hunter then ran off with his friend laughing never once looking back at her.*

Something changed that day. Hunter did everything in his power to make her next week a living nightmare. He spread rumors throughout the school about her. Every turn she took in the halls she'd hear people whispering and snickering about her.

But the nail on the coffin was the interaction the last time Abbie Collins ever saw Hunter James. He stood at the end of her driveway and looked her square in the face after she confronted him about his behavior. He let it be known, he never wanted her in any way, friendship or anything else, and it should be something she should get used to since her dad didn't want her either.

His words cut into her like a pain she'd never felt before.

And then he was gone.

The next day his house went up for sale, and she never saw or heard of him again.

But the damage was already done.

The next few weeks at school had been hell.

Until she said enough was enough. After some self-pity, she turned the nightmare at her school into drive. She begged her mom to let her be homeschooled, reluctantly her mother agreed.

Abbie then had worked her ass off. She ended up graduating early and moved right into college. She was lucky enough to intern with WCM Advertising Firm. They had loved her so much they offered her an entry-level position in the creative team and she took it in a heartbeat. There she worked her way up to Creative Director. She was next in line for the Account Executive position and she knew bringing Robert Jefferson on as a client would seal the deal.

But right now, none of that mattered.

Not one single freaking bit.

Hunter James was sitting in front of her like he knew he'd won.

She hated him. Abbie hated him with all of her being.

And the worst part was, even through all the humiliation and pain he caused her when Hunter left, he somehow took a piece of her heart with him.

Too bad she fucking hated him.

# CHAPTER THREE

HUNTER CLOSED HIS EYES.

Seeing Abbie again was like a straight punch to the gut. *Holy shit.* He'd be lying if he said he hadn't kept close tabs on her over the years.

He had.

But seeing her in the flesh was something else. He swallowed.

When Hunter read she'd graduated with honors his heart swelled for her. He *knew* she was going to make something of herself.

That was Abbie.

Abbie was always going to rule the world. He never had any doubt in his mind. He'd seen pictures of her here and there. It was kind of hard not to, considering they both were in the same field. However, those pictures did not do Abbie any justice.

Those curves.

That hair.

Those deep blue eyes.

There went that punch again.

Abbie had the silhouette of a goddess, and right now with her blouse wet, and her purple bra on display, it took every ounce of restraint in him to not jump over the table.

Holy fuck her tits were overflowing her bra.

That's when he heard a stifled cough from beside him. At first, Hunter smirked realizing he'd been caught staring, but once he registered what was going on, his fist clenched.

He wasn't the *only* one staring at Abbie's impressive rack.

A harsh wave of possessiveness crashed over him. Without even a second thought, Hunter pushed back from the conference table and shrugged out of his jacket.

He tossed it to Abbie — who was still staring at him in what he could only imagine was disbelief. Right before it smacked her in the face though, she gathered her senses and grabbed it.

"Put that on," Hunter growled. "This is a business meeting, not some after-hours red light special. Not everyone wants to see that."

That shocked her out of whatever trance she was in. If he thought her eyes showed her disdain before, he was mistaken.

Right now, Abbie's eyes looked like they'd spit fire, and they were directed right at him.

Then, to his shock, Abbie did something he never thought he'd see. She took his jacket and tossed it on the floor. "You're right, Mr. James," she spat at him, but in a calm way. "It's a business meeting. Unfortunately, this morning, I ran into a little mishap, and normally I'd have more time to change and look a little more presentable..." She shrugged nonchalantly. "Shit happens."

Abbie sent him an evil smile. "They're boobs. We've all seen them and we've all got 'em. Some are just less impressive than mine." She gave him an innocent smile. "If it's too much for you, Mr. James, you are more than welcome to wait in the other room. I'm sure once my shirt has dried, I can go over the details *I've* already acquired for Mr. Jefferson's proposal."

Oh, that was the same look Abbie had given him when they were kids and she'd thought she'd won. *Not on your life, Abs.*

Never again.

Hunter sat back in his seat. "Carry on, Miss Collins. If you've seen one tit, you've seen them all."

Her face hardened.

Mr. Jefferson laughed bringing Abbie's attention to him. "I truly apologize for my appearance," she remarked. "Since we are all adults here and I don't have another shirt we might as well go for it. Will this be a problem for you, Mr. Jefferson?"

"Please call me Robert, Ms. Collins, and also let's make sure never to tell my wife."

Abbie smiled sweetly at him, letting out a small laugh. "Deal." She gave a quick glance to her boss. Hunter could see the plea in her eyes that she hadn't just sealed her fate at the unemployment line.

Bill nodded slightly in her direction, giving her the okay.

*Showtime, Abs. Make it good.*

Abbie took a calming breath before she pulled out her laptop, causing Hunter to sit back with a huge grin on his face.

Human Resources could kiss his ass. He didn't care what lines he was about to cross. He was here for Abbie, and only Abbie. Now, to think of all the ways he could cross those lines.

Three hours later and Hunter was fucking impressed. Actually, impressed wasn't even close to what he was feeling.

Sure, he knew Abbie was good. She had to be to have gotten to where she was, but this was beyond good. Hell, it would have been the same proposal *he* would have come up with.

Abbie had every 'i' dotted and every 't' crossed. At this point, he wasn't sure what help he could be.

If Robert Jefferson didn't sign on to WCM Advertising Firm, he'd be a fucking moron.

"I like where you're going with this, Ms. Collins," Jefferson finally spoke up. "I can see where you've done your homework."

Homework? Fuck Abbie had done more than homework for this. Hunter sat back watching as Abbie stood at the front of the table more poised than he'd ever seen.

"I'm intrigued," Jefferson continued.

Abbie's face broke out into an inviting smile, while her eyes screamed bring it. "Intrigued is good. Are there any questions I can help answer for you?"

When Abbie hitched her hip, it was nearly the death of him. Hunter had always been attracted to Abbie, but now, now he was seconds from losing it. It's like each little defying gesture she made with her body went straight to his dick. Thank fuck his lower half was covered by the table.

Mr. Jefferson sat back in his chair as his hand caressed his chin. He then looked to him. "Hunter, what do you think?"

*That Abbie did a fantastic fucking job.*

The thought didn't surprise Hunter, but he knew he couldn't say it. The moment he agreed with Abbie, his chances of working with her would fly right out the window. And that was not happening — no way in fucking hell.

Nothing and he meant *nothing,* was going to stop him from finally getting what he always knew was his.

Hunter sat back in his chair and surveyed Abbie. When he looked into her eyes, he saw the dare there. The dare to tell Mr. Jefferson it *wasn't* a perfect presentation.

*Forgive me...*

Hunter looked her right in the eyes before he shrugged. "It's decent enough," he announced calmly.

Abbie's mouth dropped open in shock.

*Time to add the nail to the coffin.* "It needs work, though."

"You think so?" Mr. Jefferson looked at him nodding his head slightly.

*Here goes nothing.* Hunter squared his shoulders. "Ms. Collins' presentation was impressive to say the least; however, there are key elements she's missing, like some of the domestic dealings." He tried playing it as cool as he could, as he grasped at straws.

"This is why I wanted to bring you onto the team. We need a fresh set of eyes. Sometimes we get too complacent," Bill said clasping him on the shoulder. He then looked back at Mr. Jefferson. "I knew putting Collins and James together would be a perfect match for whatever your needs are, Robert."

Hunter turned his head toward Mr. Jefferson. "Give me a week and I'll present you with something you'd be a fool to turn down."

Mr. Jefferson cocked a brow at him. "You sure?"

Hunter looked at Abbie whose face was red and her eyes narrow. "Surer than I've ever been."

"All right then." Mr. Jefferson looked at this watch dismissing any other discussion on the matter. "My flight leaves in a few hours, but keep me posted." He stood before shaking Bill's hand. "We'll be in touch."

He then moved to Hunter. "I'm eager to see what you come up with."

When Jefferson turned to Abbie, he sent her a warm smile. "I have a feeling you and Hunter working together is exactly what my company needs."

Abbie's lips morphed into a tight smile before she shook his outreached hand. "You won't be disappointed, sir. You'll be blown away the next time we meet."

"I'm sure I will be. Especially, with Hunter now joining the project."

Hunter leaned against the back window as he watched Abbie put on the most professional act he'd ever seen.

Color him impressed all over again. She could be an actor.

"Let me walk you out." Bill waved his hand toward the door as Jefferson left the room leaving him and Abbie.

Alone.

Once they were gone, Abbie turned from where she stood staring blankly at where Bill and Jefferson had vacated and focused her eyes on him. He couldn't help the slow smirk that appeared on his face.

He only made one step in her direction before Abbie reacted.

Before Hunter knew it, Abbie was flying through the air ready to bring him down.

# CHAPTER FOUR

Abbie wasn't sure how she ended up flying through the air, hurdling towards Hunter, but she wasn't about to question it. If her old childhood antics wanted to come out and play, who was she to fight it?

Plus, he deserved it.

"Fuck!" Hunter caught her as they both plummeted to the ground. "What the fuck, Abbie?"

Throwing caution to the wind and letting her inner child take control Abbie ignored him as she hiked her skirt up around her waist, and pinned Hunter to the ground with her legs. The same way she did when they were kids.

"Get off me," Hunter growled.

"Not on your life." Abbie maneuvered herself so she could now use her right arm to pin him down at his shoulders. "I should murder you."

"You and what army?" he choked out.

A deep growl escaped her throat. Then to her utter surprise, she was being tossed through the air before landing on her back.

Shock.

She was in absolute fucking shock.

Abbie blinked in surprise, trying to understand the sudden change of events. Hunter had her completely pinned beneath him. And to her absolute horror, her legs were wrapped around his waist.

*What the fuck!*

"Now this I can get used to." The corner of Hunter's lips turned up.

Quickly and with all her might, Abbie pushed Hunter off, realizing he wasn't trying that hard to keep her there.

Hunter fell back onto his ankles.

Abbie watched mortified as Hunter then looked her body up and down. That's when she realized in her effort to destroy him, her skirt was now up around her waist and her bright pink panties with the little yellow duckies on them eating popcorn were entirely on display and Hunter made absolutely *no* attempt to look away.

*Fuck this.* Young Abbie was coming out to play again. Instantly, she launched herself back at Hunter with a war cry so fierce it *should* have scared her, causing Hunter to fall flat onto his back.

"Again? Really?" With absolute ease Hunter flipped Abbie onto her back once again. "Are we gonna do this all day? If we are let me know now 'cause I just had this shirt dry-cleaned."

Abbie clenched her teeth as she used all her might to try and flip them over.

Sadly, though, she underestimated Hunter's hold.

Push... nothing.

Push again... still nothing.

"If I pretend to let you flip me will you stop trying to tackle me?" The smug look on his face only infuriated her more.

"Over my dead body."

With absolutely no effort at all, Hunter pinned both her arms above her head with one hand before bringing his other hand to his chin, tapping it lightly. "Although, I do enjoy this view." He looked between them. "I never knew ducks liked popcorn."

As Abbie tried to fight his grip, she realized it was a lost cause. Her head flopped back onto the floor as she closed her eyes. The anger she felt coursed through every inch of her.

How in the fuck had she ended up here?

*Universe, if you're listening, please give a sister some insights and enlighten me. 'Cause right now I'm about to murder Hunter fucking James.* Abbie sighed. *Maybe if I keep my eyes closed, he'll go away. Then I can finally try and piece all this mess back together.*

"Are you giving up already? Pity. I thought you had more balls than that, Collins. At least you used too. Apparently, you've gone soft. Plus, I was rather fond of this game."

*Keep your eyes closed, Abs. Do not engage. He will eventually go away and we can pretend this never happened. I repeat, do not engage.*

"Are you ignoring me now? First, you tackle me and now you're gonna ignore me? Real mature. I guess you never grew up. And here I thought you'd be thrilled to see me."

"I must be having a stroke."

Hunter barked out a laugh as he through his head back. "Still the same old Abbie."

*Universe, it's me, Abbie, again. We just talked, but you ignored me. If you have any ounce of decency in you, can you send down a meteor right now? You know kinda like when the dinosaurs went "poof." I think I have a dollar in my purse. You can have it.*

However, the moment she felt Hunter's hands go to her hips, Abbie's eyes shot open. Quickly she tried to pull away from his touch, but to her surprise, Hunter was gently tugging her skirt back down her legs. Within seconds those little yellow duckies eating popcorn were no longer staring up at her.

Her eyes shifted from side to side trying to register what he'd done. *Okay, what fresh hell was this?*

Hunter popped back onto his feet before once again grabbing ahold of Abbie's hips effortlessly standing her up. "Up you go."

Abbie stared at him, with her mouth open.

*Is this what's it's like to have some unbeknownst blood clot go to your brain? Instead of a meteor, Universe, did you kill me? You must really want my dollar.*

Abbie's eyes followed Hunter as he adjusted his clothes before turning back to her.

His eyes brightened as he placed that godforsaken smirk on his face that instantly had her fists clenching. "Let's get started, Abbie."

Then, the fucker winked at her.

# CHAPTER FIVE

Abbie stormed into her two-bedroom bungalow with such force the wall shook when she slammed the door behind her.

"That stupid egotistical pompous mother fucker." Her fists clenched at her sides as she stomped around. "Stupid fucking Hunter James! The next time I see him I'm going to punch him right in the throat."

No matter how hard Abbie tried to calm her rage, her blood still boiled at the situation. How in the hell had her life come to this? Seriously, no please explain this?

How had she woken up only a few hours ago on one of the most important days of her career, only to be thrown into the goddamn lion's den like she was a juicy piece of meat and the lion hadn't eaten in days?

At least that's what it felt like.

It was a complete blindsided fuck you to the face.

Abbie paced the living room doing everything she could to calm herself.

After her last wrestling match with Hunter, she said fuck it and left the office. Okay, more like stormed out of the office like a tornado, but whatever. Besides, if Bill wanted to fire her for this, then so be it. Fuck him anyway for pulling this shit on her.

Actually, she should quit. Yeah, that was exactly what Abbie should do. Fuck all of them.

There was no way in fucking hell she was working alongside Hunter James.

Her head spun. She was still trying to wrap her mind around the fact he worked in the same field as her *and* in a better position. She looked up to the ceiling. "Really, Universe. Really? What have I ever done to you?" she growled as her right eye started to twitch.

*Damn it! Damn it all.*

Abbie knew she couldn't quit at least not right now. No matter how bad she wanted to. Maybe after she had Jefferson Exports under her belt she could, but until then she was stuck. And hell would freeze over, and pigs would fly out of her ass before she let Hunter take this away from her.

"Fuck!"

Abbie closed her eyes as her fists clenched at her sides. They were squeezed so tightly she was positive she was about to snap one of her nails. And she didn't care. If her nails wanted to be sissy and break with a little added pressure, then fine by her.

Stupid nails anyway.

She was done. Done with the day. Done with Bill. Done with Hunter fucking James.

Then out of nowhere, Abbie felt something tiny touch her right leg. She took another deep breath doing her best to let go of what she was feeling, there was no use in taking it out on him. She unclenched her fists. "Rup—"

Then in pure Rupert fashion, the little jerk decided he

was tired of waiting for her to acknowledge him and dug his claws into her leg. Hard.

Abbie's eyes snapped closed in pain. "Ouch, you freakin' asshole. Did you really have to do that?" She looked down at her cat who now sat on his hind legs, licking his paw as if to taste her blood without a care in the freaking world.

"You're a shit-head, Rupert. Do you know that?"

Her cat stood before going into a deep stretch. He then purposely did this weird shimmy to show off his attire.

Abbie groaned as she rolled her eyes. Rupert might be an asshole, but at least he was a fashionable asshole.

Right now, Rupert was sporting his turquoise turtleneck with his favorite rhinestone collar that had his name on it.

Seeing him do another turn, admiring himself, had the corner of Abbie's mouth lifting. Leave it to Rupert to bring all attention to him and his wardrobe. Abbie couldn't help but let out a small chuckle. It was one of the things she loved most about having a hairless cat. She got to dress him up in anything she wanted. She was just lucky enough she got a cat that wanted to be a full-on fashionista.

Rupert did another quick turn as if showing off his outfit from the other side, before going back to Abbie's legs weaving in-between them.

She bent at her waist to scratch Rupert's wrinkly head. "Are you excited your mom's home early or are you just hankering for some treats?"

At the word treats Rupert began to purr. "Figures."

Abbie rolled her eyes as she walked over to the tray she kept by the window that housed some of Rupert's belongings. Such as his princess bed that overlooked the backyard, his multiple rhinestone collars, and about one-eighth of his clothes.

When she pulled out the treat bag, Rupert started dancing around the room like a dog. That's right, half of the time Rupert acted like his canine brethren. The first time Abbie thought something was seriously wrong with him, but no. He was just really weird. So weird he could sit on command, and sometimes if he were really begging for some extra praise, he'd even rollover.

She stopped trying to make sense of him a long time ago. It was easier that way.

"Rupert, could you please *pretend* to be concerned at how bad my day was?"

Rupert meowed before eyeing her left hand holding his scrumptious goodies.

"See." She rolled her eyes. "You *are* an asshole."

He meowed stretching up on his highness legs reaching for his treat bag.

Abbie threw some of the biscuits onto the floor. *Good grief.*

Once he was happily eating his snacks, she then walked over to her bright purple couch and plopped down with a big dramatic sigh. "Today couldn't get any worse, could it?" She closed her eyes, hoping the next time she opened them this nightmare would be over.

She should have known better.

"Abbie! I know you're in there, open up!"

Her head shot to her front door as the familiar baritone voice echoed through her front room. Abbie narrowed her eyes at the ceiling. "*Really?* It wasn't a fucking request."

"I can hear you talking to yourself. Open this damn door, Abbie."

Who the fuck did he think he was? He didn't get to waltz back into her life and then make demands.

Fuck that and fuck him.

Abbie hopped onto her feet before stomping over to the door. "What the hell are you gonna do about it if I don't?"

"Do you really want to play this game right now?" Hunter's voice bellowed through the door. "You know damn well I'll kick it down. You wanna try me?"

At his asinine words, a new wave of anger shot through her. *Punch him!* Screw this. If he wanted to fight, she'd fight. "I'll fucking murder you first," she screamed her war cry as she threw open the door, ready to leap into the air.

Too bad, she should have known Hunter would've been expecting it. He caught her mid-flight before walking into the house shutting the door behind him with his foot. "You know, I think you have anger issues you need to work through," he announced strutting into the middle of the room with her in his arms. "Or, maybe you can't wait to get your hands on me?"

Abbie could hear the smirk in his voice. Just as she was about to lose her absolute mind, Hunter easily tossed her onto his shoulder into a fireman's pose.

*The asshole.*

Abbie punched and slapped at his back. "Let me down you, ass-hat. I will call the police! I will call the Coast Guard. I will call the Army. I will call your father! Watch me. Just watch me. Put me down, you ass face!"

With Abbie still on his shoulder, Hunter spun around the room ignoring everything she said. "Nice place. I always had a feeling you'd end up with something like this. It shows your personality. All ten of them."

*That mother fucker.* "Let me down now or I will cut off your balls and feed them to you!" she yelled clawing at his back.

"Do you take anything to manage your anger?" he asked

nonchalantly. "If you point me in the direction of where you keep your meds, I'll gladly get a pill for you."

Was this guy serious?

For a split-second Abbie stopped fighting him as his words registered. "Actually, on second thought, if I were you I'd never put me down. "Cause the moment you do, I'm gonna stab you with the closest object I can find."

"That could be exciting." He tossed her higher onto his shoulder as he laughed.

*Laughed.* The fucker actually laughed. How in the hell was he so fucking amused by this? Was this some sort of game for him?

Well, if it was, Abbie was going to make sure it was a game he was not going to win.

Hunter James was in for a rude awakening and Abbie was about to give it to him.

Sadly, before she could make her next move, she was tossed back through the air until she landed safely on the couch.

Abbie blinked a few times trying to regain any sense of awareness. The moment she fully registered she was out of Hunter's grasp she lunged at him.

And to absolutely no one's surprise, within seconds Hunter had her flipped onto her back, completely pinned beneath him... *again.*

Just like in the office.

"For absolute fuck's sake!" Abbie tried pulling away from him but failed miserably. How in the ever-loving hell did she keep ending up in this position? Okay, so she knew the answer to that, but she refused to place the blame anywhere but at Hunter.

No matter how childish that seemed. When it came to

him, she apparently reverted back to being ten all over again.

"How long am I gonna have to hold you still until you calm down?" He then did the thing that made her lose her last bit of sanity, if she even had any at this point.

He *smirked* at her.

"A fucking eternity." She tried her best to push him off, but he wouldn't budge.

Hunter's smile widened from ear-to-ear. "Thank god I've been putting in extra hours at the gym then."

"Is that a fat joke?" she growled at him.

For a brief second, panic washed through Hunter's eyes before he quickly shook it off. "No. If you want to be a baby about this, I'll keep you pinned under me. Eventually, you'll give." To prove his point he pushed her hands over her head, proving to her he indeed had her locked in his grasp. "Sooner or later you'll give up or you'll have to go to the bathroom. I can do this all day. The question is, can you?"

Abbie scowled. Of course, he was going to bring that up. Curse her tiny bladder. He'd remembered her one weakness.

The Collin's bladder. It only held one cup of tea before all hell broke loose.

*Asshole.*

Her eyes narrowed dangerously at him. "Why are you here, *James*? Better yet, how the fuck did you even get my address?" Mentally Abbie started scrolling through her coworkers, trying to pinpoint the traitor. She should have *never* thrown the stupid housewarming party when she bought her first home.

That's what you get for being proud of your accomplishments and wanting to share them. You get snitches. And snitches deserved stitches...

It was probably Martha in HR. Abbie bet Martha took one look at Hunter and handed him her address, bank cards, and her panties for good measure.

"I asked around," he answered with amusement in his eyes.

"And someone fucking gave it to you? Does privacy mean nothing to anyone these days?"

Hunter shrugged. "I can be very persuasive when I need to be."

Abbie pushed at his chest. "Get off me!"

"No."

She saw red. "I hate you."

"That's all fine and dandy. For a while, I hated you too. Let's move on."

That shocked her. "What do you mean you hated me? I did absolutely *nothing* to you. I'm a perfect gem. No one hates me."

"Typical Abbie." He shook his head. "If I let you go, do you promise not to kick me in the balls?"

Abbie's face scrunched. "Hmm, I hadn't thought of that..."

"Well, don't think of it now." Hunter pulled away. "I asked Bill for your address. I told him you were excited to start the project together and you had most of your notes back at your place. And, we were meeting here, but you left without giving me the address."

"So, it wasn't Martha?"

"Who's Martha?"

"No one." She sat up as she fixed her clothes that had gotten all out of place in their most recent tussle.

Once she felt somewhat presentable, okay presentable flew out the window around tackle two, but good enough she looked at him.

*Okay, Abs. Take a deep breath, a long breath. You've got this. Always remember: A Collins never surrendered. A Collins never backed down. A Collins never turned down a dare.*

*Take this one step at a time.*

She closed her eyes. Okay, first things first. Hunter was here. In her living room.

In her *freaking* living room.

No matter how hard she tried she couldn't fully wrap her head around the sequence of events that led to him actually being here. However, there was only one thing she knew for sure.

She needed a drink.

Deciding it was best to make a drink and then work all this shit out, Abbie stood and walked into her kitchen, ignoring the two-hundred pounds of muscled dick-face sitting on her couch staring at her.

She opened up her *special* cabinet the second she walked into the kitchen. She wasn't much of a big drinker, but she always had wine. Then she spotted the bottle of whiskey Ken from accounting had gifted to her at her housewarming party.

*Never a better time to start on the hard stuff then when your childhood enemy shows back up into your life.*

That sounded completely logical to her.

Quickly, she opened the bottle and took a whiff.

She'd never jumped back so fast in her life. "How does anyone drink this shit?" She blanched as her eyes watered and her nose burned.

"If you don't drink it, why do you have it?" A voice interrupted her thoughts causing Abbie to nearly jump out of her skin.

She let out an annoyed groan.

How could she have forgotten the bane of her existence was mere feet from her?

*Deep breath.* All she had to do was ignore him, and he'd go away, right? Sure, it didn't work in the office, but it was totally going to work now.

See, game plan.

That was all she needed.

That's all she ever needed. If it was one thing reading taught her, it was to go in with a plan, and you always win. Okay, it normally didn't go as planned but it always worked out in the end.

Abbie ignored Hunter as she walked over to the sink before pouring the bottle of whiskey down the drain.

She knew what she needed.

Tea.

She needed tea.

A good old piping hot cup of tea.

Tea *always* made her feel better, even when she was a child. It was something Abbie and her mother bonded over.

Her mother. How in the hell was she going to tell her Hunter showed his demon face again? Abbie closed her eyes with a sigh.

However, she quickly opened them when she felt herself being nudged out of the way as her faucet turned on.

Her jaw nearly hit the floor.

To her complete shock Hunter was at her sink *filling* her tea kettle.

She blinked a few times as she watched as Hunter turned away from the sink before walking to her stove. He then turned on the burner and placing the kettle on top.

*What the fuck?*

Was Hunter James also a mind reader now? That was

exactly it. Hunter James and his possessed demon self was a mind reader.

Her eyes widened. *Oh my god, he can read my mind. Does he know what I'm thinking now? Two plus two is what? Is what, Hunter? Answer me, you weird demon spawn you. I know you can hear me!*

Hunter looked her up and down before shaking his head.

*Oh my god,* did *he hear me?*

"Grab your cup, then let's head back to the living room so we can get started." With that, he left her standing in her kitchen like she'd been slapped.

Once she regained some of her senses, Abbie quickly scanned her tiny nineteen-fifties inspired kitchen trying to piece together what in the hell was happening and what episode of the *Twilight Zone* had she was on.

Then her eyes seemed to focus on the kettle. *How did—*

As Abbie made a step toward her stove, she heard a commotion from her living room, followed by a crash.

"Abbie get out here! You have a rat wearing a dress in your house!"

# CHAPTER SIX

"SERIOUSLY, WHAT THE HELL IS THAT?" Hunter looked at the *creature* wearing... wait? Was it wearing a turtleneck sweater? *What the fuck?* His head was spinning. Dress, sweater, it honestly didn't matter because: What. The. Fuck?

"Did you just refer to Rupert as a rat?" Abbie came storming around the corner with a cup of hot tea in her hand.

"What's a Rupert?" he asked eyeing the thing again.

"Rupert is my cat." Abbie placed her mug on the coffee table and scooped the *thing* into her arms cooing at it. "Who's a good boy? Your momma's good boy, aren't you?"

"Eww, don't talk to it like that." Hunter cringed. "Kill it."

Abbie's eyes narrowed as her lips thinned. "The only thing in jeopardy of dying here is *you,*" she huffed. "Plus, don't be rude. It upsets him."

Hunter's nose wrinkled. "Looking at it upsets me."

Abbie pointed toward the door. "There's the exit. Let the door hit you in the ass on the way out."

"Still so violent." He looked at the thing in her arms once again. "Seriously, though. *That's* a cat?" He didn't believe her. An oversized ballsack maybe? But a cat, no.

Abbie scratched under *its* chin. "Yes, Rupert is my Sphynx kitty. Or hairless kitty, whatever you want to call it."

"Do you like your kitty's to be hairless?" he asked without missing a beat as heat rushed through him as he pictured her bare.

When he saw Abbie's right eye twitch as she got the meaning of his words, his mouth morphed into his smug smirk

"Pig."

"What? It was a legitimate question." He laughed as he winked at her. Hunter then focused back on the creature in her arms. "Why's it so... weird?"

Abbie quickly covered its ears. "Don't call him weird. He's very sensitive." To prove her point the *thing* meowed.

Well, at least that answered his question that it was indeed a cat... or maybe not? At this point, the jury was still out.

"Rupert is my very special boy." Abbie murmured at the rat. "You're momma's big strong boy." She bent giving him a kiss on its wrinkly head that had Hunter gagging.

She glared at him. "You're being overdramatic."

Abbie then placed it back on the ground before fixing its sweater.

The cat had a *fucking* sweater.

Then to his horror. The thing walked right over to him. Looked him in the face and then fucking hissed.

Hunter jumped back in fear of his life. "What the fuck?"

"He doesn't like you." Abbie shrugged going back to her mug.

"I see that."

"Like mother like son, I guess."

"Put it outside." Hunter stretched out his foot, lightly pushing the creature away from him. Rupert responded with a louder hiss followed by an attack.

"Get it off me!"

Abbie brought the mug up to her lips failing to hide her smile. "No, you were mean to him. You tried to push the poor little guy away with your stinky ass foot."

"Abbie, get this thing off me!" He shook his leg trying to get the ballsack off.

Abbie was there in an instant scooping the creature into her arms. "You lay one finger on this guy and I'll rip off your balls and make you eat them. In *this* household. He ranks well above you." She pointed her finger at him. "You got that?"

"At least I rank somewhere," he mumbled.

"Yeah, right below the bin of garbage that has to go to the curb tonight," she challenged as her eyes spit fire in his direction.

"You wanna go again, Abs?" Hunter's eyes darkened. "Say the word. I'll even let you *think* you're winning for a few seconds."

Quickly, Abbie turned away her shoulders slightly slumped. "*Don't* call me that."

"Call you what?" Hunter watched as the feisty Abbie disappeared right in front of him.

What happened?

When Abbie finally turned back to him, it was a straight punch to the gut. Gone was fighting Abbie, in her place was something he'd only seen once before. His eyes squeezed closed as the memory of her standing in her driveway appeared.

When he opened them, he saw Abbie throwing walls up around herself.

"Abs," she repeated. "Don't call me Abs."

Hunter always called her Abs. At least when they weren't fighting he did.

"Abbie..." he said softly moving closer to her.

"No, it's fine." Abbie put her hands up in surrender before she headed toward the back of the house.

For a moment he just stood there trying to make sense of what the hell just happened.

*Fuck it.* Quickly Hunter followed behind her. That's when he saw her open the door that led toward the backyard.

"Come, Rupert. Out you go." The cat - in all his turquoise glory - trotted right past Hunter and out the back door.

*The hell?* He cringed away.

Sure, he knew seeing Abbie again wasn't going to be easy, but right now he was positive he was in some warped version of hell that was ruled by a rat in a dress.

Deciding it was best to go along for the ride he followed after them.

However, the moment he stepped outside he was taken aback. He did a quick double-take around the place, and an instant feeling of unease swept over him. It was something straight out of a horror movie.

Everything was dead.

And he meant everything, even the grass.

There were raised garden beds along the back patio, but yeah, those were all dead too.

It was terrifying. "What the hell happened out here?" Had the apocalypse happened and he missed it?

Hunter scanned his surroundings once more. That's when he spotted it. There was *one* potted plant on top of a patio table that still *looked* alive.

Well, kinda.

"What do you mean?" Abbie cocked her brow.

"It looks like something out of a, *you better run 'cause I'm gonna murder you and wear your skin*, kinda thing out here."

Abbie's eyes hardened. "Do not make fun of me!"

"I'm not making fun of you, Abbie. I'm seriously concerned here. Compared to the inside of your house this place looks like a fucking mortuary."

Abbie huffed before crossing her arms. "I have a hard time keeping plants alive, okay?"

Hunter pointed at the semi-living one on the table. "So, you bring them out here to show them your death garden and what awaits them?"

Abbie ran over to the plant covering its leaves as she'd done with the rat. "Don't tell him that. He's gonna be my survivor. I know it."

Hunter scoffed as he walked over to her and the plant. "It's already turning yellow."

"Shut your face." She picked up the pot before she spoke to it. "You're gonna be just fine. Don't listen to stupid head over there."

"I think I just saw it shudder." Hunter plucked the plant from her hands before sticking his finger in the soil. "Abbie, this thing is dry as a damn bone. When was the last time you watered it?"

"Yesterday?" Her face scrunched.

Hunter shook his head. "Try again."

"Uhh, maybe three days ago."

He arched his brow.

"Okay fine. I have no idea. Maybe a week ago." She grabbed the plant from him, placing it back on the table. "I'm trying, okay? I really am." She walked over to the hose at the back of the house and turned it on. She then walked over to the plant on the table and at full blast tried to water it.

"Fuck, Abbie!" Hunter snatched the hose from her hands before kinking it sending her a "are you out of your mind" look. He then lightly began dripping the water into the pot. "Are you trying to drown it now?"

"Don't make fun of me! I love my plants. I love them a lot. Just looking at them makes me happy! I really try. I don't know what happens. Jeez, as soon as I bring them home, they just die. It's like they hate me." Abbie started hyperventilating as she threw her hands all around. "I talk to them. Pet them. Sing to them. I try to remember to water them. I love them! I want them to live, but they just die."

Hunter's hand flew toward her garden. "So, you keep the ones that didn't make it for what? To add to your garden of death?"

She clenched her teeth. "Fuck off. I'm trying, okay? Plants make me happy. I want them all around. I used to keep them in the house, but when they die I feel bad so I'd bring them out here and hope... I don't know to somehow revive them."

"What do you mean you *pet* them?"

She shrugged. "You know, I pet their leaves."

He stared at her.

"It's not weird, okay? I read somewhere if you give them love they will love you back and flourish."

"There are so many things wrong in that sentence I'm not going to even try and decode it."

"No one asked for your opinion on my botany skills."

"What skills?"

"Asshole." She stomped back to the house before shutting off the hose. "Who died and made you the plant police?"

"Apparently, the plants."

"Fuck you."

"Name the time and place."

"Pig."

"Plant killer."

Her fists clenched at her sides. "Take that back."

"It's the truth. Look, even your rat stays out of the garden. It probably knows the second he steps in there it's game over for him."

"Leave Rupert out of this."

"I will if you promise to never buy another plant again. Even I don't want to see them die. Hell, I bet the plants are so excited to finally be going home, but the second you take them out here they scream and realize what stage of hell they were just brought to."

"I'm gonna murder you."

"You keep saying that." Hunter wound up the hose before placing it back where it belonged. He then grabbed the somewhat alive plant and walked back inside.

"Where are you going with that?"

"Inside."

"It belongs out here. It needs the sun." She ran after him.

"Actually no, do you see how yellow it is on this side?" He pointed to the leaves. "You're giving it too much sun. Essentially, you're burning it to death."

Abbie froze as she stared at him. "I am?"

"Yeah. Didn't it have a little marker in it when you bought it telling you how much light and when to water it?"

She shrugged. "Maybe? Rupert likes to take those things and play with them."

*Figures.* He shook his head. "Next time, stop him. This plant only needs moderate sun." He walked back into her kitchen, removing some of the knickknacks Abbie had on her windowsill above the sink.

"Keep it here." He placed the desperate plant on the ledge. "That way it will only get *some* sun throughout the day but you'll also remember to water it." He turned to her with a pointed look. "But don't water it for at least two days. We just gave it a huge dose. You don't want to drown it."

"You can't drown plants. They're plants," she mumbled turning away.

"Say's the woman that's drowned half the death garden out there."

"Stop calling it a death garden!"

"What else would you call it?" He cocked his brow.

"Whatever," she spat as she walked toward the back door. "Rupert. Inside."

Instantly, the little rat came running back into the house. His turquoise sweater was the only thing Hunter got a glimpse of as it ran by.

A shiver ran down his spine. That thing gave him the freaking creeps.

Abbie stepped in front of Hunter with her arms crossed and a pout on her lips. "I *guess* seeing that you aren't gonna leave anytime soon. We might as well get started on this project. A project you know damn well was perfect and you only said it wasn't because you once again want to ruin my life."

*Ruin her life?* Was she out of her mind? The day he walked away from her had sent his world into a downward spiral.

Abbie had it wrong.

She was the one that ruined *his* life. He was just finally man enough now to do something about it. Okay, well it helped his boss told him to stop pussyfooting around and go for it but still. He was here to change that.

Deciding it was best not to lay all that at her feet, though, he did the one thing he knew would get a rise out of her.

He smirked. "Sounds good to me."

Hunter had to hold back his laugh when he saw Abbie's eye twitch.

She then mumbled something under her breath that he couldn't quite hear but was pretty sure had the words "fuck face" and "ass-hat" in it.

"I guess we can go over my notes." She shook her head as she walked past him and to the living room, grabbing her bag on the way. She then pointed to the couch. "Have a seat. Do you want anything to drink? Water, tea, arsenic?"

"The arsenic does sound lovely, but I think I'll stick with water."

"Pity." Without another word, Abbie headed toward the kitchen.

Knowing she wasn't looking his way, he admired her backside until she was out of view.

*Shit.* It got better and better each time he looked at it.

She had an ass that begged to be squeezed as he rode her from behind. Hunter groaned as images pierced through his mind.

Fuck.

His dick hardened against his zipper. He needed to stop doing that. He wasn't some snot-nosed kid anymore.

Cursing his lower half, Hunter grabbed his bag he'd brought with him and headed to the couch. When he saw the rat sitting there, he nudged it with his bag. "Off."

Rupert looked at him blankly.

"Seriously, dude, Off. You freak me out."

Rupert stood slowly and looked Hunter in the eyes. Then the thing turned its head over to the window. Hunter, a little freaked out at the turn of events, cast his eyes to whatever had drawn the freakishly large scrotum's attention.

That's when he saw the yellow bag with the words "cat treats" on it. He looked back at the rat. "Are you kidding me?"

Rupert meowed.

"I don't negotiate with terrorists."

Rupert meowed louder, stretching out his long body in one of the creepiest sights Hunter had ever seen.

"Holy shit, if I give you a fucking treat will you leave me alone and fly back to your mothership?"

Rupert meowed again but this time he started licking his paws. "You win. Damn." Hunter walked over to the treats. To his horror, the moment he picked up the bag the rat began jumping around like a damn dog.

"What the hell is wrong with you?"

"Nothing," Abbie yelled. "He's mommy's perfect little boy." Abbie appeared from around the corner. "Tell him to sit. He will."

"No shit?"

"He's a very smart boy."

Hunter looked at the thing. "Sit, you disgusting rat."

That was exactly what the thing did. Albeit, it gave him an evil eye while it did.

A cat sat on command. "Holy hell."

"Told you he was smart. Now, let's get this over with. I have better things to do than to spend my time with you." Abbie plopped onto the couch, pulling out her notes.

*I can think of things to do* with *you.* Deciding it was best not to get kicked in the balls today, Hunter grabbed the pad of paper he brought with him and sat next to her.

About forty-five minutes went by while they went over in detail the information Abbie had researched on Jefferson Exports.

Then he heard it.

He could swear he'd heard the same noise at *least* three other times. Deciding to ignore it once again he focused back on Abbie's voice.

*Pop.*

"All right, what the hell is that popping I keep hearing?"

Abbie ignored him as she continued explaining the overseas exports.

"What the hell is that? I've heard it at least four times now." Hunter started looking around the room, everything looked normal except for the rat that sat on the glass coffee table licking its paw.

"It's nothing." Abbie picked up her mug and took a sip before placing it back down.

Hunter narrowed his eyes. "What aren't you telling me?"

"Really, it's nothing." She shrugged as she picked up her

mug again taking another small sip of tea before placing it back down. "I found out something after getting Rupert."

Hunter's eyes shot to the rat in concern. "Found out what?" *That it was an alien sent here to kill everyone?*

"When hairless cats sit on things sometimes they suction themselves to the surface."

Hunter dropped his notepad as his mouth flew open. "They *what*?!"

"I don't know why you are making this a big deal?"

"A big deal? Are you telling me that *things* asshole suctions itself to shit? And then it fucking pops when it gets up?" Hunter stared at the rat in total disbelief.

"They're called asshole kisses and if you don't like them, you can leave. You know the way out."

"That's gross as fucking hell, Abbie. Are you telling me you're constantly surrounded by asshole *kisses*?"

"It's why I keep cleaner on hand *and* it's only on some surfaces," she defended as she shot a death glare in his direction. "You do gross shit too. Rupert can't help it. He didn't ask to spread his asshole love everywhere. It's just who he is."

"Are you hearing yourself right now?"

"Of course, I am. I'm the one saying it. And trust me, when I first found out I was a little freaked, too. But then I realized it was a part of him. It's not going to stop me from loving Rupert."

"And you didn't think about getting rid of it? That would have been my first thought. He leaves 'asshole kisses', Abbie. That's not normal."

Abbie turned to Hunter with shame in her eyes directed right at him. "Give him away? Wow, you haven't changed one bit, Hunter James." She shook her head before reaching out for Rupert. "Why would I ever make him feel like he's unwanted? Just 'cause he has some weird, albeit gross issues, I'd never abandon him. The moment he came into my life he was my family. Through thick and thin. I'd never make him feel like he wasn't worthy enough to be loved for who he is." Abbie pulled Rupert into her lap before giving him a squeeze.

Hunter instantly felt like a dick. He knew the exact reason Abbie would never turn him away. Hell, it was probably the same reason she hadn't forced him out of her home.

Abbie never wanted anyone to feel as unwanted as she did when her dad abandoned her and her mom.

*Great move, asshole. You keep racking up the points, now don't you?* Hunter cursed himself at his stupidity. He watched as Abbie held onto to Rupert as if her life depended on it.

*Perfect.*

At that moment, something broke inside of him for Abbie. He watched the woman that he would do anything for cling so desperately to a disgusting alien, scrotum looking, rat thing.

As Hunter opened his mouth to apologize though, all hell exploded.

The cat who was once calm decided to let its true colors show. The colors of a fucking demon that it was. The thing started flailing around, hissing, trying to escape.

"Really! I feed and *clothe* you!" she screamed as the rat flew out of her arms leaving Abbie holding her left arm tightly. "You know that purple nightshirt you had your eyes on?" She yelled at the cat. "You can eat shit. No way in hell am I buying it for you now. Dick."

Hunter burst into laughter causing Abbie to turn toward him. "Shove it."

Hunter — through his hysterics, scooted over to Abbie

grabbing her arm to examine it. "I'm glad to see it's not just me on the receiving end of your fire."

"You can eat shit too." She tried pulling back her arm but Hunter held onto it tightly.

"It looks like he got you good." She had a few cuts up and down her forearm.

"I've had worse. Try being startled awake by a naked cat that gets spooked 'cause a branch hits a window." She turned her angry eyes back to the demon on the coffee table looking at her like *she* did something wrong. She turned back to Hunter. "He sleeps at my head to keep warm. I had to go into the office explaining to everyone I got into a fight with a hairless pussy that thought my face was the enemy."

Hunter barked out a deep laugh. "Oh, man." His hand went to his stomach as he tried to control his amusement. "I missed you, Abs."

It was like all the air in the room was sucked out. As soon as the words were out of his mouth, all the laughter died. He sat up and stared into Abbie's eyes and for the first time since seeing her again, he saw pain.

It was worse than a punch to the gut this time. It was like something he'd never felt before. "Abbie..."

Abbie looked into Hunter's eyes and no matter how hard she tried she couldn't turn away. Hearing his nickname for her once again hurt. There was no other way to put it.

It was like it sucked all the air out of her lungs and then kicked her in the stomach for good measure.

"You know, Hunter, it's been a long day. How about we pick this up tomorrow? Let's meet in the conference room at eight."

"Abbie..."

She couldn't look at him.

Not when she needed to get herself back together. Right now, her heart hurt so bad, she was positive she was actually having a heart attack. What else could explain it?

Deciding it was her heart's issue and *not* the feelings she'd pushed so far deep inside of her coming to the surface again, she made a mental note to call her doctor.

Taking a deep breath, she tried to calm herself. "I'm tired, Hunter. You can't deny it's been a day for the books." When she opened her eyes again he was staring at her.

Sorrow written all over his face. To her surprise though, he nodded. "Tomorrow morning," he said softly.

"Yeah." She gathered her notes, shoving them back into her bag as Hunter did the same in silence.

Slowly he walked over to her front door. However, he paused when his hand touched the doorknob. He turned to her. "Tomorrow."

All she could do was nod.

He stared at her for a few seconds before turning away and walking out the front door. Once he was out of sight Abbie closed the door and fell back onto it.

She wasn't one hundred percent sure what happened, but she knew damn well she wouldn't let it happen again.

She closed her eyes as she felt her heart shatter. Just as it did the last time she saw him. She couldn't explain why her heart did weird things for Hunter, but it did.

And that wasn't going to do.

This was the one and only time she would let her guard down when it came to Hunter James.

Abbie slid down her door as she tried to get her head to stop spinning.

Rupert must have known something was wrong. He

climbed into her lap, purring as he made himself comfortable.

Abbie scratched under his chin. "How am I going to survive this, baby? How am I ever going to make it out still intact?"

# CHAPTER SEVEN

THE NEXT DAY, Abbie walked into the conference room with her head held high. After her little freak out last night, she did some soul searching and remembered who she was.

A Collins never surrendered.

A Collins never backed down.

A Collins never turned down a dare.

She had this.

Abbie would take each moment one at a time and when the proposal was over and they landed Robert as the newest client of WCM— which she was positive would happen. She'd leave.

At first, she wasn't going to quit, but after some serious thinking last night, it was the best thing for her.

Hell, maybe at this point she could start her own advertising company.

Who knew where she'd end up; but she did know for sure there was no way in hell she would work alongside Hunter James.

Last night she even drafted her two-weeks notice letter and put together a tentative business plan.

She loved WCM Advertising. They'd given her so much in her career, but this wasn't something she was going to stand behind.

Her mother always said she was destined to take the world by storm. Sure, Abbie always thought her mother was full of crap. You know, all that, my kid is going to change the world and stuff, but now she believed it. She could start her own advertising business.

And the more Abbie thought about it, the more she liked the idea.

Her clients loved her. Abbie had always made it her mission to sell them on *why* they should choose *her* to help represent what they need rather than signing on with WCM just to sign on because of the name.

Abbie was a master at selling potential clients the journey they would go on together. It's how she moved up in the company so fast. And that was exactly what Abbie would do on her own.

Away from Hunter James.

As she rounded the corner, she froze dead in her tracks the moment Hunter came into view. He sat there with his jacket hangin on a nearby chair and his sleeves rolled up a few inches. He was looking over his paperwork spread out across the conference table.

He was gorgeous.

Actually, gorgeous was an understatement.

Her stupid heart did that flip thing. She placed her right hand onto her chest trying to calm herself.

*On your lunch break call your doctor dumb-dumb. This isn't healthy.*

Then Hunter, sensing she was there, looked up and smiled.

*Holy freaking hell!* She almost fell backwards. How was

it possible for someone to walk around that good looking? Wasn't there some cosmic law against it?

Abbie took another deep breath and squared her shoulders. *You've got this, Abs. You can survive anything. You've got your plan. Stick to it.*

She walked through the door with her head held high. "Morning."

Hunter beamed at her. "Mornin', Abbie. How did you sleep?"

She cocked her eyebrow at him. "As good as I ever sleep with a naked cat trying to suffocate me to steal my warmth."

Hunter tilted his head to the side. "Naked pussies keep me up at night too."

"Pig."

"Starting the venom early, I see."

"With you, always." Abbie walked over to the table. "What are you working on?"

Hunter looked at her. "My lunch order. What do you think?"

Before she knew it, Abbie broke out into a smile. A genuine smile that soon matched Hunter's as they said at the same time. "Lunch order."

They both laughed as Abbie pulled out her laptop. "What's on the menu?"

Hunter tossed her one of the papers he'd been looking at. "How do you feel about Italian?"

Abbie looked down at her shirt.

"Are you asking your boobs?"

"No. I was checking to see what color blouse I had on."

"Are you sure, cause it kinda looked like you were asking your tits? Better yet, do they respond to anybody? Let me ask them?" Hunter walked around the table and stood right in front of her.

That's when Abbie's heart skipped again. And to her horror, she felt her nipples peak. *Apparently, they respond to you.* Abbie scoffed at herself. *Bad body. Bad boobs. Remember what we talked about last night body? None of this shit today.*

Hunter leaned towards her chest. "Are you okay if we order Italian for lunch?"

Abbie took a step back while pushing at his chest. "Do not talk to my ta-tas, dick-wad."

"Why not?"

"First, that's weird as hell. And second, I wasn't *asking* my chest. I was really checking to see what color shirt I had on."

Hunter looked her up and down. "What does the color of your shirt have anything to do with it?"

"You won't get it." Abbie let out a dramatic sigh.

"Try me." Hunter crossed his arms over his chest.

"Fine." She narrowed her eyes at him. "But if you by *any* chance make a smartass remark, I will tackle you to the ground."

That stupid smirk appeared on his face. "I'll try my best. Although, that doesn't sound like a punishment to me."

"Pig." Abbie laughed. Somehow even in the weirdest most bizarre situations with Hunter, she found herself feeling this weird ease. "I needed to make sure I was wearing a darker color. Nine times out of ten I drop something on my shirt during lunch. Okay, anytime I eat. My boobs sit there like they have a target right in the middle and food *always* nails its mark. If I'm having Italian the probability goes up to twelve out of ten times."

"I don't think you understand statistics."

"I don't think you understand having huge boobs and

expensive shirts that cost an arm and a leg to get dry cleaned."

Hunter nodded. "You're right, I don't understand having boobs but I do know how to excite them."

"Pig."

"You say that a lot."

Abbie shrugged. "Call 'em as I see 'em."

Hunter reached out and flipped the bottom of her blouse. "Does dark purple meet your unneeded approval for Italian?"

Abbie looked down at her top again. She knew at this point it was beyond a shadow of a doubt she was going to spill something on it. Was this top worth the hassle of dry-cleaning?

"Jeez, women are complicated." He rolled his eyes. "It's settled we're having Italian. I'll buy you a new top if I have to. Now, let's get started."

"Bossy."

Hunter looked her in the face as something weird passed over him. "If that's what you like, I have no problem ordering you around."

Heat flashed through her.

*Stop it. Stop it, stupid body! I mean it!*

"Pig."

"I'm starting to think pig means something different to you." He tapped his finger to his chin. "Actually, the more I think about it the more I can only come to the conclusion it means sexy in your world." Hunter winked. "Now when you call me pig, I know you really mean sexy."

"Ass-wipe."

Hunter turned giving Abbie his backside. "I do have an extraordinary ass, don't I? It's all the hours at the gym."

"Blah." Abbie shuttered in disgust. "You said an icky word."

Hunter cocked his brow toward her.

"Gym. Eww. There is nothing good at the gym."

"I beg to differ. "

"You would." She rolled her eyes. "I bet you wake up at two in the morning and spend three hours there every day. No, thank you. I'd rather sleep. Or eat, or get a root canal."

Hunter looked her up and down. "Are there other ways you like to work out your body?"

The tension in the room thickened.

"Like killing your plants?" Hunter threw his head back in laughter and just like that the tension was gone.

"Asshole."

"There you go thinking about my ass again."

"Yeah, I'm thinking about kicking it."

"This is gonna be fun." Hunter smirked as he pulled out the seat in front of Abbie. "Let's do this."

# CHAPTER EIGHT

THE KNOCK on the conference door had Abbie nearly jumping out of her skin. "What the hell?" She looked behind her.

Since settling into the project, Hunter and Abbie and gone over everything she had done so far. At first, she was still resistant to work with Hunter, but after the first hour, she let it go and put her head down.

Sadly, no matter how bad it hurt to admit, Hunter did have some good ideas. She now saw why he was an Account Executive. Her respect for him went up. Just a little bit, though, no need to get crazy here.

Hunter was still an asshole.

"Food's here," Hunter announced as he grabbed the bag from the carrier and brought it over to the table.

"When did you order?" Her brows shot to the ceiling. "Better yet, what did you order? I'm one hundred percent positive I was never asked what I wanted for lunch."

Hunter's face broke into the stupid smirk she hated. "You were the one that said you liked to be ordered around. I was just giving in to your hellish demands."

"Hellish demands? Are you insane?" She held up her hand. "Wait, don't answer that. You're completely insane if you think the conversation from earlier resulted in me liking to be ordered around. You need to have your head examined." Abbie stood before reaching into the white paper bag to see what Hunter had ordered.

"That's exactly the way I heard it. It's not my fault you don't communicate well." He smirked at her again.

That same fucking smirk she wanted to rip off his face. After letting out a small huff of annoyance, Abbie pulled out the first box as a wave of garlic hit her. She peeked inside.

Garlic knots.

Her mouth started to salivate. She freaking loved garlic knots.

Abbie placed it next to her and moved to see what else he'd gotten. Box after box she began to pull out.

Eggplant Parmesan.

Penne Alla Vodka.

Lasagna.

Spaghetti with meatballs... *Yuck.*

First, Abbie hated ground beef and secondly, if you are going to go to an Italian place get something with more pizzazz. She put the lid back on the box and pushed it toward the other side of the table. "Blahh."

"With that look of disgust on your face, I take it you aren't a fan of the simple stuff in life?" Hunter chuckled reaching for the discarded box.

"Meatballs are gross."

"Not *my* meatballs."

Abbie shot her eyes to him. "Pig."

"Sexy."

Abbie faked a gag. "I'm gonna vomit." She shuddered

before opening up the last box. "Calamari! My favorite." Without a second thought, Abbie popped two rings in her mouth.

She didn't even try to suppress the moan that escaped her lips. *God, Calamari is so good. Thank you, Universe, for making these little dudes and then deep-frying them.* Another moan left her lips as she danced from side to side in pure joy.

However, when Abbie opened her eyes, Hunter was staring at her with a pained look on his face. "What?"

Ignoring her question, Hunter pulled out his phone.

"What are you doing?"

He didn't look up from his device as he answered. "Placing an order for five more plates of Calamari."

Abbie rolled her eyes as she laughed. "Make sure they add extra marinara."

Hunter froze as his eyes went to her.

"What? I'm not going to deny myself food I love to eat."

Hunter's brows pulled together causing the corner of Abbie's mouth to turn up. She sent him a wink as she popped another one into her mouth. "I know you aren't ordering it."

His brow rose. "How do you know?"

Abbie tapped her finger to the side of her head. "Intuition."

"More like witchcraft. You say the word and I'll order you a truckload." Hunter slipped his phone back into his pocket. "I like a woman that knows what she wants."

"Right now, I want to eat. I hadn't realized the time. I can't believe I lasted this long not trying to kill you."

"I have to admit I'm disappointed you went a whole four hours and not even once attempted to tackle me. You've lost your edge."

Abbie ignored him as she placed her hand back in the carrier searching for the silverware. Then she pulled out a plastic bag. Thinking that's where the forks were, she opened it.

"Fuck you." She turned her evil glare to Hunter who was now doubled over in laughter.

"Your face," he said as he tried to control himself.

Abbie pulled out a piece of cloth. "Did you *really* get me a bib?"

In between his gasps for air, he choked out in hysterics, "You were so concerned about your shirt."

"Idiot."

*Whatever*. As she looked down at the bib, she fought her smile. "Boobs." Abbie looked back at Hunter. "How did you find one that said boobs?"

His eyes danced with mischief as he answered. "You'd be surprised at some of the weird sayings they put on baby shit these days. I was shocked."

"And when did you have the time to peruse the baby aisle."

"When you were going over the online campaign for the tenth time."

Abbie rolled her eyes, throwing her hair into a bun on top of her head and placed the bib around her neck.

When she looked back at Hunter, she couldn't help but smile at his shocked face. "Didn't think I'd wear it did you?"

"To be honest, no."

Abbie winked before she motioned to her shirt. "Gotta protect the goods." She pointed to the bib. "Just like the thing says."

Hunter sat back in his chair as he watched in amazement while Abbie wore that stupid bib and ate her lunch. She was constantly surprising him.

It was like no matter what he did to get a leg up on her, she'd do something just as insane to throw him back down a notch.

Which was also a testament for just how damn good of a worker she was. As he went over the proposal she'd already done, he was more and more blown away. Abbie Collins was a master at what she did.

"Stop staring at me," she said as she wiped marinara sauce off her chin. "Hey, look." She pointed at the bib. "This came in handy."

Hunter looked at where she pointed and sure enough, there was a glob of sauce right in the middle.

"Why don't they market these to adults?" Abbie pulled off the bib. "They should."

"Put together a marketing plan for it. You can be the spokesperson." Hunter laughed.

Abbie squared her shoulders as she lifted her chin at him. "Maybe, I will."

With a shake of his head, Hunter pushed away his spaghetti and meatballs. "Where are we?"

Abbie moved her food to the other end of the table grabbing the last ring of Calamari tossing it into her mouth.

When she moaned the sound went straight to Hunter's lower half.

*Fuck,* she needed to stop doing that.

She might have had the urge to tackle him when he got under her skin. Well, he wanted to tackle her too.

Instantly, images of Abbie spread out on the conference table in front of him clouded his mind. He'd gladly feast on her, and he was positive he'd moan the exact same way she did when she placed a piece of Calamari in her mouth when her taste finally touched his tongue.

"Are you constipated? You're making weird noises." Hunter's eyes shot open to see Abbie giving him a strange look.

"Are you gassy? It was probably the meatballs." She pointed to the box "Meatballs are disgusting."

"What do you have against meatballs?"

"I'm not a fan of ground beef."

He cocked a brow. Abbie was strange, but he wouldn't have it any other way. Doing his best to push aside the images of her spread-eagle out in front of him, he grabbed his computer and tuned it toward her. "All right, we have one week to get this proposal done. Bill told me when I came into the office this morning, Jefferson will be back Tuesday."

Abbie's brows knitted together. "He didn't tell me that."

Hunter shrugged, winking at her. "I said I'd let you know."

Abbie sent him a dirty look before she let out a dramatic sigh. "Let's just forget everything and work. The sooner we get this over with the sooner we can part ways. "

*Part ways?* Over his dead body. Hadn't she figured out *she* was the only reason he was even here?

It would be a cold day in hell before they parted ways again.

He just needed her to realize that.

And he would stop at nothing until she did.

# CHAPTER NINE

IT'D BEEN an intense few days working alongside Hunter, and as Abbie walked into her living room with a piping hot cup of tea in her hands she headed directly to her couch.

She planned on plopping down on that thing and never getting back up.

She'd been looking forward to today. It was going to be her Saturday to do nothing. Her day *away* from Hunter.

And she needed it. Being so close to him had drained everything inside of her.

Settling into her spot, she looked over to see Rupert curled up on the side of the couch in his black turtleneck lined with gold trim. It occurred to her, he had the right idea.

Abbie stretched out her legs causing Rupert to meow in annoyance. "Hush your face."

Rupert huffed in disapproval before turning away from her.

"No skin off my nose," she said as she grabbed the remote and surfed the channels for morning cartoons.

Abbie glanced over at the pile of paperwork she had on the coffee table. When she arrived home last night, she went over what they'd done to see if she'd missed anything.

She took a long sip of her tea cursing Hunter.

It didn't matter.

Thinking about him right now was pointless. This was her day - Hunter free. And she was going to enjoy every last second of it.

Then as if the Universe wanted to mock her, there was a knock on the door.

Abbie groaned as she pushed herself up. "It better be one of those neighborhood kids selling cookies. That's the *only* person I'm opening this door for." She placed her mug on the coffee table before slowly gathering her strength. Still only half awake she walked over to the door and opened it.

"Morning, sunshine." Hunter pushed past her.

"Oh, for fuck's sake."

He turned toward her. "I like the way you greet me." Abbie watched as he looked her up and down. "Nice outfit."

That's when Abbie's eyes fully shot open completely alert. She looked down at herself. *You've got to be kidding me?* She was in her t-shirt nightgown that went to just below her butt, no bra. Hell, she wasn't even wearing panties. But that wasn't the issue, nor was it that her hair was an absolute mess.

It was what her nightgown said.

"Don't you wish you had a hairless pussy just like me," Hunter read her shirt out loud looking at the hairless cat smack dab in the middle of it. "Do you have a hairless pussy, Abbie?" Hunter asked with a strain in his voice.

*Thank you, Universe, you once again have made me*

*want to climb up there and strangle you.* Abbie closed her eyes. *Just a few more days Abbie that's all you have left.*

She opened her eyes. "Yep. He's right over there." Abbie pointed to Rupert. "Please excuse me while I go change. I didn't think you'd be an inconsiderate asshole and show up at my doorstep unannounced. Silly me, I should have known that was your M.O."

"Don't change on my account." Hunter's eyes were honed in on her chest.

"Pig." Abbie stormed past him and up toward the stairs.

"All I'm hearing is *sexy*."

"Eat shit." Abbie started making her way up the stairs. She only stopped when Hunter gave a loud whistle.

She turned to face him, crossing her arms over her chest as she sent an evil look in his direction. "What?"

"Let's just say I'm not the only one with a nice ass."

That's when she remembered she wasn't wearing any underwear. Quickly, Abbie pulled down her nightshirt. "Pig."

"Sexy." The corner of his mouth lifted. "Now, I know what not to buy you for your birthday. And here I was scrounging the internet for sexy panties."

"Fuck you."

"Name the time and place."

Abbie looked past him. "Rupert, attack." She sent a silent prayer to the Universe when Rupert meowed.

The moment she saw Hunter jump she smirked. "Serves you right." She turned on her heel and climbed back up the stairs.

"Abbie, tell him to stop. He's coming toward me!"

"Sorry can't hear you." Abbie laughed.

❀

*Holy fuck!*

Hunter moaned as the image of Abbie's ass floated through his mind. It was the smallest little hint of cheek as she walked up the stairs, but it was enough to send him into overdrive. And those thighs.

He groaned as his dick pushed against the zipper of his pants.

*Fuck me.*

At this point, he was sure he'd have a permanent mark etched into his dick.

Then Rupert let out an ear-piercing meow.

"Holy shit! Back demon rat. Back." Rupert stopped his progression toward Hunter only to lift his paw and lick it. "Jeez, dude, you're creepy."

As quickly and carefully as he could, Hunter walked around the cat keeping his eye on him at all times. Once he was safely past the rat, he walked into Abbie's kitchen shaking his head. He grabbed the kettle and within seconds had the water on the stove, bringing it to a boil.

Hunter then started going through her cabinets looking for mugs and tea bags.

He closed his eyes. *Abort, abort.*

His eyes shot back open. Every time he closed his eyes, he saw her walking up the stairs now.

*Fuck me twice.*

How the hell was he going to survive being so close to Abbie and *not* touching her? He had to get his head in the game. There was no other way around it. He came to WCM Advertising on a mission. And when this was over, Abbie was damn well going to know why he was back.

Hunter looked around the kitchen trying to distract himself from the image of Abbie's ass. He zeroed in on the plant.

He rolled his eyes at its appearance. When he walked over to it, he stuck his finger in the soil and realized it was bone dry. *Again*. "What am I going to do with you, you habitual murderer of plants?"

With another eye roll, he gave the thing water and contemplated taking it with him when he left.

It would have a better chance.

After a few more minutes the kettle began to sing. He poured the water into the mugs before he made his way into the living room. That's when he saw what was on tv. "Cartoons, really?"

Rupert jumped onto the coffee table startling him. "The fuck." He almost spilled the mugs as the rat gave him the eye.

"Don't be mean to him," Abbie snapped as she came around the corner. "I'll throat punch you if you are."

He cocked his brow at her. "When you were upstairs did you take your anti-violence pills?"

"Screw you."

Hunter turned away from her walking to the couch. "I'm guessing that's a no."

"Did you make me tea?"

He turned back, handing her the mug. "Yeah."

Abbie stared at it blankly. "But I already had tea."

Hunter looked around and saw the mug on the coffee table.

*Shit*. He wanted to smack his forehead. *Good going, idiot. Of course, she already had tea. This is Abbie after all*. Without really thinking about it, he took her old mug and downed it in one gulp. "Now, you don't."

"What is wrong with you?" Her brows shot to the ceiling.

He wanted to know the answer to that, too. Because right now he was at a loss for why the fuck he just did that.

When he said nothing, Abbie walked over to him. "Thank you." She took the mug. "I'm not sure if I should throat punch you for going through my kitchen, though."

"So violent."

"Only around you."

From the corner of his eye, he surveyed her. She'd changed into black leggings and a maroon shirt that had the words "Do Everything with Love" across the chest.

She'd also thrown her hair into a messy bun on top of her head again, which he now realized was her go-to style.

Fuck him, she was beautiful. Even when she wasn't trying to be.

"Mmhhmm. There is nothing like tea," Abbie moaned after taking a sip.

Hunter couldn't help but wonder if she sounded the same in bed. "Sex is better."

"Says you."

He looked at her with a challenge "Let me know when you want me to prove it to you."

"You know, you've gotten perverted in your old age." He saw her failing to hide her smile behind her mug.

"And you've become a prude."

"Oh, Hunter, Hunter, Hunter." She shook her head as she looked at him with a wicked smile. "I am *far* from a prude. If you only knew."

Well, this had taken a turn in a direction he liked. "Oh, really?"

"Yes." Abbie winked at him before shrugging. "But you'll never know the secret drawer I keep in my bedroom or meet my past conquests."

*Fuck me. Secret drawer?* His mouth dried as his eyes

darted to the bottom of the stairs. Her bedroom was only a few steps away.

As he was about to say something he heard a crunching. A loud crunching. Turning around, he saw Rupert at the corner of the coffee table making a full meal out of their work. "What the hell?"

# CHAPTER TEN

WHEN TUESDAY MORNING ARRIVED, Abbie was ready. With only a few more surprise incidents with Hunter, they'd nailed out every detail.

Abbie was surprised to find she worked really well with him. Better than she'd worked with any other of her other co-workers.

Last night they had stayed well past midnight hammering out the last details and going over absolutely everything for this morning.

Abbie looked down at her watch. She was right on time. They'd planned on meeting thirty minutes before the presentation to go over everything one last time.

And that was all that really stood in her way of freedom. A few measly hours and she was done.

Abbie had this. She was a majestic goddess.

Robert Jefferson was going to sign on the dotted line today, and then she'd walk right into Bill's office and hand in her two-weeks notice.

She was ready for a challenge.

Nothing and she meant *nothing* would screw this up for her.

As Abbie turned into the office, she had her head held high and her shoulders squared.

"There's been a problem," Bill announced as she walked into the conference room. *Well, that was not what she was expecting.*

"What problem?" She heard Hunter say as he walked in behind her.

"Yeah, what's going on?" Abbie asked, as Bill started shuffling around before he pulled something out of his pocket. "Unfortunately, something has delayed Robert."

Bill was acting weird. Actually, it was more than weird, after all the years she'd worked with him he'd never been this fidgety before.

"Okay, no meeting today then?" Abbie asked.

"Sadly, no." Bill glanced around the room before looking back to Abbie. "However, Robert's in a bit of a time crunch."

"Okay..." Hunter crossed his arms over his chest. And as Abbie watched him, she sensed he knew something was off. When Hunter looked her way, it was confirmed. Something wasn't sitting right with him. "Does he want us to do a video conference or something?" he asked Bill.

"Not exactly."

"What do you mean not exactly?" Abbie turned her attention to her boss who was now looking down at the papers he'd pulled out of his pocket. He then held them out.

"What's this?" Abbie took a step forward grabbing it. However, the moment she got a good look at it, her heart stopped. As in full-on, she was ninety-nine percent sure she was having a heart attack. "Plane tickets? *Plane* tickets!"

"He wants this done and now." Bill straightened as she looked at her.

"Plane tickets!" Abbie yelled in a complete panic.

Hunter ever so calm, nodded his head as he examined one of the papers he was now holding while Abbie was losing her ever-loving mind.

"The flight leaves in four hours." Hunter looked at her. "That's doable."

Abbie was past freaking out now, she was in a full-on panic attack. "That's doable? That's not doable, Hunter. That's beyond *not* doable. That's so far in the un-doable column I can't even see it." Was Abbie breathing, she couldn't tell if she was breathing? She scanned the room as the walls felt like they were closing in on her.

Hunter cocked his head to the side as he watched her with his left brow arched. "What's got your panties in a twist?"

All the color drained from Abbie's vision.

"Abbie doesn't fly," Bill answered.

"You don't?" Hunter hadn't taken his eyes off her. She didn't know whether it was the concern he had on his face or the fact her heart died, but somehow words finally formed. "No, I don't fly." Sweat broke out on the back of her neck. "Humans aren't meant to fly. If we were, we would have been given wings, dumb-dumb. That's not a hard conclusion to come to." She pointed at herself. "I don't fly."

"People fly all the time."

"I'm not one of them. You hear me?"

"How do you think I got here? I flew. I fly all the time, Abs."

Abbie crossed her arms over her chest as she fought the urge to lunge at him. "Well, I don't."

Hunter, mimicking her stance, cocked his head at her. "You are today."

"The hell I am." She pushed out her chest. *You wanna go? We'll go. First, I'll fight you, then I'm kicking Bill's ass. Watch me.*

"Fine," Bill stepped in and looked at Hunter. "Do you think you can present this proposal on your own?"

*Are you fucking kidding me?* Abbie's head was about to pop off. "Wait? Hold up. Are you out of your mind? Are you really willing to send *him* out on this? The guy that just came onto the project a *week* ago? Screw that!" she spat. "You're not sending him to do this alone. Not after everything I've done."

Bill shrugged like it was absolutely no bother to him. "You're leaving me no choice, Collins. Robert wants this done now. That's it. If you can't get on the plane then I'm sending Mr. James."

Abbie's mouth fell open in complete shock. It was like Bill Michaels had slapped her clear across the face. "This has got to be a fucking joke." Abbie looked around the room. "Where are the cameras? I'm on some prank show right?"

Bill shook his head. "Enough. It's either you and Hunter go together or Hunter goes alone. Either way, someone is getting on that plane and headed to Florida."

"Why can't we drive?" she whined, as all the hard work she'd put in slowly slipped away from her.

"Across the country?" Hunter cocked his brow. "Come on, Abbie, you know we can't."

"Shut up!" she spat. "You have no say here."

"Actually, I have a lot to say." Hunter walked over to her. "This is happening, it doesn't matter if you like it or not. I'd rather do it *with* you since you know Jefferson Exports inside and out, but if I have to, I will go alone."

Abbie jaw hit the floor. This wasn't just a slap to the face this time, no this was well beyond that.

"I *want* to do this with you, Abbie. Make no mistake in that. You are the *only* one qualified to make this proposal," he pleaded with her.

As she looked into Hunter's eyes, something shifted inside of Abbie. Amongst all the chaos she was feeling along with the betrayal. Abbie saw a trust in his eyes. She didn't know how, or why, but it's what she saw.

And beyond that trust, she saw anger. But not at her, no, she saw anger at the situation.

Well, at least that made it a little better. As she stared Hunter in the eyes, she took a deep breath.

She needed to get herself together. If she was serious about branching out on her own, she couldn't let something like an airplane stop her.

No.

That was never going to happen.

A Collins never surrendered.

A Collins never backed down.

A Collins *never* turned down a dare.

And she saw it. She saw the dare in Hunter's eyes.

"Fine. Fucking fine, fine, fine!" She pushed past him as she pulled out her phone. "Let me call my mom, maybe she can look after Rupert. Oh, shit, I need to get home to pack. Wait, what should I pack? When are we coming back?" She looked at the ticket in her hand. "Oh god, these aren't round-trip tickets." She looked at her boss. "Why the hell not?

"I figured it would be better to leave it open-ended what if Robert has questions? I'm giving you a corporate card for all of your expenses and tickets back." He pulled out his wallet.

"He can pick up the damn phone and call." Had her boss jumped on the crazy train?

"Abbie, you're my top employee but this is out of line."

"You're out of line." Abbie's fist clenched at her sides. Just when she was about to lose it, she felt someone place their arm around her shoulders and start to lead her out of the door.

"We've got this," Hunter announced. "First, we'll head to my hotel and grab my bag then head to Abbie's and leave from there." Hunter held her close to his side.

*What fresh hell was this?*

Abbie looked over her shoulder to see a huge smile on Bill's face. "I knew I could count on you, Hunter."

*Let me at him!* However, no matter how hard she tried to break out of Hunter's hold he held her tight. "Down, killer."

"I'll murder you all," she snarled.

"I know." He pulled her a little tighter to his side.

"I knew I could count on you," Abbie mumbled, which only made Hunter laugh.

How in the world was she going to survive this?

Once they made it to the elevator, Abbie shrugged out of his embrace. That was the last thing she needed right now.

Once they got inside and the door closed Abbie looked at her reflection as she heard the beeps as they descended.

*Planes crash. Planes crash and the people on them don't survive or if they do, they end up on some deserted island where they need to make homes out of bamboo and then pray they don't get eaten by islanders.*

People aren't meant to fly in planes. People aren't meant to fly period.

"You're shaking." Hunter wrapped his arm back around her.

"And you're a dumbass."

Hunter let go before taking a step back from her, crossing his arms over his chest. "You know, you'd think after a week of this shit, I'd be used to it by now. Seriously, it's just a flight it's not a big deal."

"It is to me." She was breaking inside.

"It's gonna be fine. Plus," He smiled at her. "I'll be there the whole time."

"That doesn't reassure me."

"It should."

"Why?"

"If something happens, I'll be there to protect you." Hunter puffed out his chest.

"Great. That's exactly what I need. Some big strong man that thinks he can protect me."

"You think I'm strong?

"Shove it."

Hunter threw his head back in laughter. "Gladly. Come on, my hotel is only around the block. Then we can swing over to your place and get what you need."

Abbie's heart raced at the fear of her impending death. "Fine. But I'm gonna complain the whole time.

"At this point, I wouldn't expect anything less."

# CHAPTER ELEVEN

HUNTER WATCHED as Abbie ran around her house cursing under her breath as she *tried* putting together a bag.

Tried was an understatement, though. It was more like a tornado Abbie had come to play. She was running up and down the stairs with clothes in her arms. She'd then throw them on the couch before going through them. It was like clockwork.

He looked down at this watch. *Three...Two... One...*

"Shit." Then she was off again up the stairs to get what he assumed was more clothes? He honestly had no idea, what was going on.

It had been the same sequence of events for the last forty-five minutes.

All he knew for sure was Abbie had somehow short-circuited.

Hunter looked to his left. The rat must have thought so also since it sat next to him watching its mom lose her shit.

He then heard a thud come from above him, followed by the words, *motherfucker*.

"You okay up there?"

Rupert had taken notice as well since his ears had perked and was now staring at the top of the landing.

"I'm fine," Abbie answered in a huff. "Just fell over?"

"Are you sure? That sounded like a question."

"Am I sure I fell or am I sure I'm fine?" she yelled back.

"Both." Shaking his head, he looked back at the rat. "Time to go check on your mom and see if I need to call for reinforcements. You know, the ones with white jackets."

Rupert meowed causing Hunter to shudder. Deciding to ignore the thing he started up the stairs. They only had about two hours before they had to be at the airport and from what he'd witnessed the only way there were going to get there on time was if he intervened.

As he walked up the stairs the rat escorted him. He was probably just as concerned for his mother as Hunter was at this point.

Once he got to the top, he looked at the oversized scrotum. "Which way?" The rat in a bright pink turtleneck ran past him in and into the door on the right.

*Okay, that way.*

Following behind him he stepped into the room.

It was way worse than he thought.

Abbie was on the floor amongst a pile of clothes, shoes, and lord knew what else. "Abbie?"

"Oh my god, get out. You can't see this," she mumbled from beneath a pile.

"See what?"

As she jumped to her feet, the mountain of clothes she had piled on her bed toppled over on her causing her to fall back onto her ass.

That explained why he kept hearing her fall over.

With a chuckle, Hunter walked over to Abbie. He effortlessly grabbed her waist hoisting her into the air before placing her on the edge of the bed. "Has anyone ever told you, you freak out?"

"Screw off."

He looked around the room. "What happened in here?"

"I don't know. I started pulling out a blouse I thought I would need then I realized I didn't have a good pair of pants to go with it. So, I started looking for a skirt. Then I realized what if I forgot to pack something or what if I leave something behind I might need? Then I started going through everything I own and tried to make sure I didn't forget something important. What if I forget to pack a bra? I can't walk around with my tits flopping all over the place. I'll probably give myself a black eye," she rushed out.

Damn, she was adorable when she freaked. And lucky for him, that was Abbie's permanent state. He had to fight the urge to bend down and kiss her pouted lips.

Hunter's gut clenched.

He could still remember the kiss he'd shared with her sixteen years ago. Something over took him as he slowly leaned forward.

Then Rupert bit his ankle.

"What the fuck?" He jumped back.

Abbie looked behind him. "He doesn't understand what's going on. It's normally really clean in here. He probably thinks we're having an earthquake."

"So, he bit me?"

Abbie shrugged as she resumed going through the remaining clothes on her bed. "He thinks you caused it."

Hunter glared at the rat staring at him as it licked its lips. "The fuck?" A chill went down his spine as he turned back to Abbie while also keeping a close eye on the *thing*. "Let's take a deep breath, okay? First things first, where is your suitcase?"

"Downstairs in the hall closet. That's why I was bringing my clothes down there."

His eyes widened. "Please tell me you're not planning on trying to pack all that shit down there are you?"

Abbie's eyes swam with tears causing his heart to break for her. She was so vulnerable right now. Without fighting it, Hunter leaned over and kissed the top of her head. "I'm gonna get your suitcase. Why don't you call your mom now and tell her what's going on? That way you can ask her to take care of the rat? I'll meet you downstairs once you're done. Okay?"

To his surprise, she nodded completely helpless. He didn't like this Abbie. No. He'd rather take her threatening to unman him every second than this Abbie.

Before he did something stupid like kiss her, he turned on his heel and jogged out of the room.

She must really hate flying if she was freaked out this much. Although, she had an aversion to keeping her cool when it came to him, she was always organized and ready for anything. This wasn't the Abbie he knew.

No, this was an Abbie that was terrified beyond belief. And all he wanted to do was take her in his arms and kiss away her worries.

Hunter ran down the stairs and quickly made his way over to the kitchen turning the kettle on. *Might as well give her something to calm her.* He then walked over to the hall closet and retrieved her suitcase.

At least he could do this for her. He placed it on the coffee table and started going through her clothes on the couch.

As he worked through what she had, he heard a chomping. Hunter then turned only to see Rupert was now sitting *inside* the suitcase staring him down as he chewed on the side.

"What the hell is wrong with you?"

The cat meowed before it looked over at its treats.

"Jeez, dude." Hunter walked over to the bag and watched as the rat danced in a circle. "Sit."

Rupert did it without hesitation causing Hunter to cringe away. He then looked at the princess bed and shook his head.

At this point, nothing surprised him anymore.

He tossed some treats onto the floor keeping the rat occupied. He moved back to the couch. "Well, if I'm gonna do this, I might as well start with the most important things."

The corner of Hunter's mouth lifted as his eyes honed in on a pair of lace purple boy shorts. "Panties it is."

Abbie took a deep breath as she looked around her room. It was a mess. No, mess wasn't a word to describe it, it was a disaster.

Just like her.

She had absolutely no idea why or how she'd lost her mind, but here she was in the middle of World War three in her bedroom.

Abbie knew she was being overdramatic. There was absolutely no reason for her to be acting like this. *Especially,* in front of Hunter.

She cringed. She didn't even want to think of the fact he'd been a witness to all of this. She figured she could deal with that later though, first things first, she needed to call her mom. It only took two rings before her mother answered.

*"Baby! What do I owe the pleasure of you calling in the middle of the day?"* her mother sang from the other end of the line.

"Hey, Momma." Abbie toyed with the bottom of her shirt.

*"Abigail, are you okay?"* her mother's concerned voice came through the phone. *"You don't sound okay. Are you sick? Oh baby, you're sick. Okay, I'll be there in twenty minutes I just gotta go to the store and get the fixings for soup."*

Abbie's heart swelled at her mother's words. Her mom was always trying to take care of her. Even if most of the time it was done in an overreaction.

That's when it hit her. She rolled her eyes.

Abbie was doing the same thing. She placed the palm of her hand on her head. "No, Mom. I'm not sick. But I need to ask you for a favor."

*"Are you sure you're not sick? Something sounds off."*

"I'm not sick, Mom. I need to go away for a few days and I need for —"

*"Go away where? What's going on?!"*

Is this how she sounded when she freaked out? Dear god, she hoped not. "Calm down, mom. The project I've been working on needs to be presented in person. My flight leaves in two hours."

*"You're going to fly?"*

"Yes." Her voice sounded small even to her.

*"You're terrified of flying. You always say people aren't meant to fly. Are you sure you can't drive?"*

"I already asked. And no, we can't video conference apparently. The client wants an in-person meeting." Why they had to be there in the flesh Abbie still had no freaking clue. Tears welled in her eyes.

*"Oh, baby..."*

"It's going to be okay, Mom." She wiped away her tears. "I just need you to take care of Rupert and my plants."

*"What plants? Do you have any living right now?"*

"Mom..." She rolled her eyes.

*"What, it's an honest question? Of course, I'll take care of them, even the dead ones."*

"As a matter of fact, I do have a plant living. It's in the kitchen right now. Hunter saved it."

*"Who's Hunter?"*

Abbie's heart dropped as she realized what she'd said. *Oh shit.* "Uhh, gotta go, mom. Flight leaves in two hours. Bye."

*"Abbie, don't you dare hang up this phone! Wh–"*

Abbie threw her phone across the room like it was on fire. "Shit. Shit on all the crackers." Slowly she walked over to her phone like it was a bomb about to go off. And with the number of chimes it was sounding, that could be at any second.

Carefully she picked it up only to see text after text coming in.

*Did you really hang up on me? Your own mother!*
*Is Hunter your boyfriend?*
*Why did he save your plant?*
*Why didn't you tell me about him?*
*Is he treating you right?*
*Should I have a talk with him?*
*Answer me, Abigail Collins. I will drive over there right now. Actually, that's what I'm doing. I'm getting in the car.*

Abbie quickly sent a text back.

*Jesus, Ma. No, it's not like that. To make a long story short, which I promise to call and explain about later, but it's Hunter James.*

Abbie smacked her hand to her head after hitting send. "Really? Why did you say that?"

Her phone instantly chimed.

*AS IN HUNTER JAMES FROM YOUR CHILDHOOD?!*

Damn it! Damn it straight to hell. She swallowed as she sent the next message.

*Yes...*

Abbie turned off her phone. You can't have your phone on while in flight anyway. She was just starting early. That was her story and she was sticking to it.

*In flight...*

She gulped. Oh god, she was about to board a flying death machine. This was it. This was how she was going to die.

Just as her panic started to resurface, she remembered Hunter was downstairs. Abbie looked to the ceiling. "Really, Universe? Fucking really? Am I a joke to you?"

Quickly she hopped up from the bed and left her room not caring that she'd have to deal with the mess when she got back.

As she raced down the stairs she saw Hunter going through her clothes before picking up one of her shirts. He then folded it before placing it neatly in her suitcase. "What are you doing?"

Hunter turned and looked up at her. "Packing. What does it look like I'm doing?" He sent her an arrogant smile.

"You're packing *my* clothes?"

"No, I dumped mine out and wanted to re-pack." He quirked a single brow at her. "Of course, they're your clothes."

"You can't pack for me." She crossed her arms over her chest.

"I already did." Hunter placed another item, which looked like a shirt. "You've got four business shirts. Two skirts, one pair of black and one pair of brown pants." He pointed to the suitcase.

"What?"

As she stared at him in disbelief, his face beamed in amusement. "Six pairs of panties and two bras." The fucker then pulled out a purple polka-dotted bra. The *same* purple polka-dotted bra from the day the jerk walked back into her life.

Watching it dangle on his finger made her snap. Before she knew it, she was in the air, her target acquired.

# CHAPTER TWELVE

*T*HIS ISN'T SO BAD.

Abbie closed her eyes as she felt the plane pull away from the gate and head toward the runway. *Yeah, this is easy. We're just driving right now. Driving to the runway. That's safe. Driving is on the ground.*

Nothing to see here. See, she was fine.

Abbie looked to her right to see Hunter staring at her in concern. There was a part of her that wanted to send him the finger, but there was a bigger part of her that was relieved he was there.

After tackling him to the couch, he quickly turned the tables on her. Hunter had ended up flipping them over and somehow gotten her pinned to the floor after the pile of clothes — including them, avalanched off the couch.

After making sure she was okay, he then promptly secured her arms over her head...again.

*Bastard.*

That was also the same moment her heart did that stupid flippy thing again as she looked up at him. Abbie didn't know what the hell came over her when it came to Hunter but she didn't like it.

And no matter how bad it pained her, she was glad he was there. It might sound silly but the fact he took the decision away from her with packing, actually helped quite a bit.

When he finally let her up, Abbie was ready to go through the packed items and tackle him all over again. But once she saw what he'd packed in her suitcase, it was like all her tension was released.

She was impressed.

Hell would freeze over before she told him that, though. Instead, she glared at him for touching her panties to begin with as she walked to the bathroom and grabbed her toiletries. When she came back out, he handed her a to-go cup of tea. Her heart had done that stupid flip *again*.

She took the tea as she tossed her stuff in her bag. It was a sweet gesture.

Probably filled with poison, but sweet.

Abbie had given Rupert a big kiss on the head and told him his grandma was coming to check on him and to not have any wild parties or at least if he did to not get the cops called.

The ungrateful jerk only blinked a few times at her before going back to sleep.

Good to know where she ranked on his importance scale. That nightshirt was definitely being removed from her online shopping cart.

"Not so bad, right?" Hunter asked, distracting Abbie from her thoughts.

She turned to him and forced a fake smile on her face. "Sure. We haven't left the ground yet."

Abbie insisted Hunter take the window seat which

honestly didn't matter to her. If the plane was going down, it was going to go down regardless of where she was seated.

Although, if something *did* happen, she wanted to be in the aisle seat. Rest assured she would be the first one off this bitch if something went down.

She glanced at Hunter. Her boss had booked them in first-class giving each row only two seats. It gave her more legroom, which she was all for.

Hunter stretched out with a sigh. "If a plane is gonna have an issue, it normally happens when it takes off or lands."

Her body froze as her heart raced. "We're about to take off."

"I know." He smirked at her.

"Asshole." Abbie's palms began to sweat as her mind raced with all the bad things that could happen.

Then out of nowhere Hunter reached over and grabbed her hand giving it a squeeze. "It's gonna be okay, Abbie."

Her eyes filled with tears as she looked at him. "How do you know?"

"I promise you nothing will happen." When Hunter looked her in the eyes, it was like he could see into her soul. And, for some strange reason, she believed him.

He squeezed her hand tighter. "It will be over in a few minutes."

"What will be over?" Abbie panicked as she looked around. Her heart plummeted. She knew what was coming.

She closed her eyes.

Death.

Death was coming her way.

"The take-off, Abbie. Relax." He squeezed her hand again causing her to look at him.

"I can't relax. Not when I'm about to die!"

Hunter chuckled. "Close your eyes, Abs. I'll let you know when it's safe to open them."

Without even questioning it, she did what he said. Well, she also prayed to the Universe and squeezed the ever-loving crap out of his hand.

*Holy fucking shit!*

Don't get him wrong. Hunter was ecstatic he was holding Abbie's hand, but with her Sumo Wrestler death grip she had going on, he was pretty sure he'd lost all circulation in his fingers. Looking down at their conjoined hands and seeing how purple they were he was positive of it.

"We're clear for take-off," came over the intercom.

"Oh god, oh god, oh god." Abbie squeezed his hand tighter. "Hunter, we're gonna die."

*Oh, fuck.* He thought he felt a bone break. "Shit, Ouch. Where the hell is this strength when you're attacking me?" Hunter groaned moving to see if he had any feeling left in his fingers.

"Yes, we are," she ignored him. "We totally are. We're gonna die and then I'm gonna be some weird floaty ghost that can only haunt this plane and that's gonna suck 'cause I'll be forever cursed to fly."

"If you're dead, it won't matter if you fly."

Abbie stared at him horrified. "Don't say that."

As Hunter realized she had no intention of loosening her grip, he cocked his brow. "You can say you're gonna die but I can't?"

"No, you can't! You're supposed to be the sane one between us. Don't you know that?"

"You're admitting you're being overdramatic, then?"

She stared at him blankly. "Have you met me?"

"My bad." Hunter held up his other hand in surrender.

"If I die, I'm not haunting this plane, I'm haunting *you*." Her eyes narrowed on him. "That settles it. I'm gonna make your life a living hell as your permanent ghost."

"Wouldn't we both die?" He fought his smile at her horrified look.

"Not if I have anything to say about it!"

"You've got some serious issues, Abs." Hunter shook his head.

"And you're annoying."

Hunter pulled their clasped hands to his mouth before kissing it. "At your service."

"Eww. Don't do that!" Abbie finally released his hand in a frantic move before wiping the back of her hand on her pants.

"You're welcome." He shrugged as he opened and closed his hand to see if it was broken.

Abbie gasped snapping her head to his. "I'm welcome? For what? Your nasty germs? No, thank you!"

Hunter pointed out of the window. "We're level."

In a split-second Abbie was crawling over the seat and him. She had both her hands in his lap as she strained her neck to see.

He felt the heat of her hands on his thigh.

*Fuck.*

"Holy shit. Oh my god, Hunter, look how high we are. You can't even see the ground." As she pushed to get closer to the window one of her hands slipped between his thighs causing a groan to escape him.

She must not have heard. Especially, since she was still trying to get a better look out the window. Abbie spread her fingers getting a better grip as she pushed more of her weight on his thigh.

Abbie's pinky finger was only millimeters from his growing dick now. He snapped his eyes closed. It took everything inside of him not to buck. *Fuck me.*

Abbie turned toward him. "How high do you think we are?"

Hunter's eyes shot open. Her face was so close to his, he lost all his ability to speak.

He needed her.

Fuck waiting. He needed her and he needed her now.

He started to lean in...

"Ma'am, I'm going to have to ask you to get back into your own seat," a voice snapped Hunter out of his trance.

"The Captain hasn't turned off the seatbelt sign."

Hunter turned to see a perky flight attendant beaming at them.

Abbie jumped back into her seat with a shout. "Ahh, sorry."

The flight attendant smiled at Abbie sending her a knowing wink. "No need to apologize, hon. If my husband looked like him, I would never get out of his lap."

Abbie's face drained of all its color. "Oh, he's not—"

"I'll make sure to keep her in line next time," Hunter interrupted sending the flight attendant a matching grin.

"Dominant." The woman's face lit. "I like it." With a wink sent in Hunter's direction, the flight attendant left.

Abbie turned to him with a death glare in her eyes. "What the hell? Why did you do that?"

"Do what?" Hunter shrugged before turning back to the window.

"Make her think you're my husband."

"It's not a big deal, Abbie."

"Not a big deal? Not a big deal!"

"If you tackle me this time, she'll think we're fucking." He smirked at her.

Abbie stared at him astonished. "You're a pig."

A chime came over the intercom. "You are free to move about the cabin."

"And, you're safely in the air." Hunter smirked. "You're welcome."

He watched as Abbie sat back in her seat a little confused and pissed.

Score one for him.

As Abbie sat there plotting his death, which he was sure of, Hunter closed his eyes and worked on calming himself.

From Abbie being mere millimeters from his dick to the flight attendant assuming they were married...Hunter's heart raced.

He turned to look at Abbie who was still plotting; however, his eyes scanned down to her left hand and honed in on her ring finger.

*Soon...*

# CHAPTER THIRTEEN

"And that is why, if you don't go with WCM Advertising, Mr. Jefferson, you're an idiot." Abbie squared her shoulders as a bold smile spread across her face.

For a brief second Hunter was taken aback, but when he looked over at Robert, he had the same smile on his face Abbie had.

*Holy shit! Well done, Abbie!* Hunter nodded at her.

Once again, Abbie never ceased to amaze him. Now, he personally wouldn't have gone as far as to call Robert an idiot, but Abbie had balls.

A huge set.

She'd always had.

As Hunter watched her, he fully took her in. Abbie was in her element and she knew it. There was a glow around her. Not one hair out of place, her makeup was subtle but accentuated her features. She looked so professional you would have never guessed four hours ago she was crying as the plane landed, nor that she changed in the airport bathroom, and did her makeup and hair in the cab on the way over to Jefferson Exports.

Abbie was fucking amazing.

"An idiot?" Robert chuckled. "Strong words there, Ms. Collins."

Abbie shrugged. "I will always shoot from the hip, Mr. Jefferson. There is enough bullshit in the world already. If more people put aside the niceties and spoke the truth, we wouldn't have to constantly be wondering if what we're doing is the right thing." She turned to Hunter. "I'll be the first to admit I didn't think I needed Mr. James' assistance on this proposal, but after his help with tightening up the loose ends. No one can deny this is one hundred percent the solution your company is looking for. With all do respect, if you don't sign on the dotted line today, yes you *are* an idiot, Mr. Jefferson."

*Holy shit.*

Hunter didn't know what to process first. The fact Abbie admitted working together was a *good* thing or how her absolute bottom line confidence in telling Robert to sign or fuck off, turned him on so fucking bad he was about to come in his pants?

*God damn.*

Robert looked over at Hunter. "Do you agree I'd be a moron not to sign?"

"Without a doubt." Hunter didn't hesitate as he looked back at Abbie. "She's right. You won't get what you're looking for anywhere else. You and I both know that."

Robert sat back in his chair as he placed his hand on his chin. "I don't think anyone has ever dared to call me an idiot outside of my wife."

Abbie smiled as she winked at him. "Women know these things, and a few select men."

Robert threw his head back with a laugh. "Sold."

Abbie pushed the contract across the table toward

Robert. "Once you sign, Mr. James and I will head back and gather a team to start producing what we discussed."

Robert dropped his pen before looking at her. "I want you in charge of that team." His face hardened. "If you can't guarantee me that right now. No deal."

A moment of brief panic washed over Abbie's face before her walls shot up. No one would have noticed, but Hunter knew her. He could read her like none other.

"I'm not an Account Executive, Mr. Jefferson. Mr. James over here is, but I can reassure you I will play a huge roll in your portfolio. I can promise you that."

Robert didn't look pleased with her words. Actually, he looked pissed. He sat back in his chair and narrowed his eyes at both of them. "I want to make this clear right now," he said. "I am not signing on with WCM Advertising. I am signing on with *you*. Whatever you have to do to make that happen, I'm fine with. But keep that in mind. I will *always* have enough money and enough resources to break any contract I bind myself into. You got that?"

"Understood." Abbie walked around the conference table and stood next to Robert holding out her hand. "I won't bullshit you. It's what I pride myself on. If anything happens, I will personally call you. Until then, I can assure you, I've got your back. Same with Mr. James." She looked at Hunter.

"I second that."

"Good." Mr. Jefferson flipped over the contract one more time and signed on the dotted line. "I'm looking forward to working with you both."

"Likewise," Abbie remarked walking back to the other side of the table.

Hunter watched as Abbie gracefully collected her belongings.

"Now, you too better hurry," Robert chuckled. "I'm surprised Bill sent you out here with the threat of the hurricane. He knew I was fine with waiting until the storm had passed."

Hunter snapped his head back to Robert. "What? What did you say?"

Before Robert could answer, Abbie's bag flipped over as she stood there shaking. Instantly, Hunter was at her side picking everything up. When he looked into her eyes, he saw the pure terror staring back at him.

Mr. Jefferson bent over picking up some of the scattered papers. "Yeah, we have a Category One Hurricane right off the coast. It's projected to hit in a few hours."

"*Is that why it's so dark out?*" Abbie yelled as the papers in her hand started to shake. "I know it rains here all the time so I didn't think much of it. Oh my god. A hurricane! Like a full-on blow your house down hurricane?"

"We get them all the time here," Mr. Jefferson announced. "No need to be worried as long as your flight leaves before the storm, you'll be fine. I'm sure you won't even hit turbulence."

*Shut up. Shut up!* Hunter screamed in his head looking at Robert. *Shut the fuck up.* His attention moved back to Abbie. Holy shit, she'd gone completely white. *Fuck.*

Hunter scooped up the remainder of their stuff. "Thanks, Robert. We'll be in contact." He grabbed Abbie's arm and pulled her out of the room.

"I'm looking forward to it," Mr. Jefferson called from behind them.

"Breathe, Abbie, breathe." She was in a complete daze. "A little weather never stopped anyone. Our bags are already packed. We didn't even book a hotel."

Anger coursed through Hunter as he clenched his teeth.

"Now I know why Robert was surprised we called telling him we landed."

"Why in hell did Bill send us here in a fucking hurricane?"

Hunter wanted to know the answer to that too.

"Technically, he didn't send us in a hurricane. He sent us *before* a hurricane hit." As soon as he could, he was going to call Bill and rip him a new asshole.

"He lied to us! Bill said Robert had to have this presentation *now*. He said I had no choice but to get on a fucking airplane. A plane, Hunter. A freaking plane. Bill knows how terrified I am of flying and to find out we flew into a hurricane and he knew!" Abbie started shaking. He didn't know if it was from fear or anger, but he was right there with her.

"Trust me. I'm just as pissed as you are."

"Are you, though? Are you? You're not deathly afraid of dying, Hunter, I am. We could have driven! Fuck. I bet at this point Robert would have been fine with a fucking video conference. Why the hell would Bill do this?" Her face hardened as she shook.

"I don't know, Abbie, but as soon as I can I'm calling him."

"Fuck you calling him, I'm gonna fly back there right now, rip off his balls and make him eat them!"

There was the Abbie he knew. If she was spouting violence, she would be fine. "Let's worry about it later. Right now, we've gotta get to the airport." Hunter pulled out his phone. "I'm booking us the next flight back."

"Good."

Once they made it out of the building Hunter glanced around. The sky looked angry and now that he realized it, the wind had also picked up.

He hadn't even thought to look at the weather when they left. It all happened so fast and with Abbie freaking out, she became his only priority.

Shit, Hunter cursed himself. If he had only taken a second to check the news he would have realized what was going on and put a stop to it.

As Hunter made arrangements on his phone for a car to pick them up, he heard Abbie sigh. "It's not Bill's fault."

"Yes, it is."

"I get it," she said. "He probably only saw Robert signing on. Even though it's completely fucked up, with Robert pushing back he needed to make sure to secure him. He probably didn't think of anything else."

Hunter stared at Abbie in shock. "That's very insightful, Abbie."

Her mouth curved into a smile. "I'm still gonna throat punch him, though."

Which caused Hunter to let out a laugh. "I'll hold him down."

"Deal."

Abbie did her best not to freak the fuck out. Deep breath in, deep breath out. There was no use in losing her shit, anyway.

It was already decided. Whether Hunter was signing on to WCM or not, she was putting in her notice. Screw trying to be the new Account Executive.

Everyone could eat a bag of dicks for all she cared.

This was her sign from the Universe. Abbie was meant to branch out on her own. Especially, after what Robert said. He was only signing on to work with *her*. Not the company.

That was all the proof Abbie needed that she could do this. It was her philosophy that had clients trust her, not just because they could put together some state-of-the-art advertising and make some silly apps for them.

No. It was what she brought to the table.

Regardless, none of that mattered right now. Abbie's only thought was getting the fuck out of the east coast.

A hurricane? Holy freaking shit.

Yep, she was going to throat punch Bill. That was one hundred percent for sure.

However, before Abbie could plot Bill's death the car Hunter called pulled up. As it stopped next to the curb, Hunter ran to the back tossing their bags in the trunk. He then walked to the back door opening it. "Can you get us to the airport?"

"That's why I'm here," the driver said with an amused smile.

Hunter pushed Abbie's back guiding her into the back of the car.

As she scooted herself to the opposite door, she looked out of the window. It didn't look good. Actually, it looked horrible. The sky kept getting darker and darker and the wind was now blowing consistently.

"Are you sure you all want to head to the airport?" the driver asked catching Abbie's attention once they were on the road.

"Yes," Hunter answered. "Our flight leaves in an hour."

The driver shook his head as he looked at them through the rearview mirror. "Are you sure about that? Last I heard, about five minutes ago the Governor declared a state of emergency. All flights are grounded."

*A state of emergency?* Abbie's heart dropped. *Oh god, we're gonna die. This is it.*

"That can't be right." Hunter pulled out his phone. "I just bought these tickets. They wouldn't have sold them to me if the flight was grounded."

"Hey, I'm just relaying the info. I'll still take you there." The driver shrugged, but Abbie saw his smile in the mirror.

She turned her gaze to Hunter as panic filled her. He must have sensed it since he reached out and squeezed her hand. "It'll be fine, Abbie."

"They say it's a bad one. The stores have been cleaned out for days," the driver announced. "Hell, I tried to get some extra water this morning and the shelves were so empty, I had to walk right back out of the store."

"If it's gonna be so bad why are you working?" Hunter snapped.

The driver looked back at him in the mirror. "For numb-nuts like you. There is always a few that think the storm is nothing." He pointed at the meter. "Plus, it's prime money for me."

"Are you kidding me?" Abbie's eyes widened.

"Bill's paying for it, so who cares?" Hunter squeezed her hand tighter.

Abbie sat back on her seat. "Fine." *Make that two punches to Bill's throat.*

"On that bit of knowledge, let me jack up the cost per mile now," the driver laughed.

"Double it," Abbie scoffed.

"As you wish, my lady." The driver readjusted some stuff on the screen. Once he was done, he put the front window down and whistled.

A few minutes later they pulled into the airport and

they all got out. As Hunter turned to pay the driver, he held out his hand. "I'll wait right here for you."

"What do you mean you'll wait?" Hunter cocked his brow.

"Chances are you're gonna go up to the check-in desk and they're gonna tell you all flights are grounded. I can take your money and go if you'd like, but seeing how deserted this place is, I doubt you'll get another ride to a hotel. The closest one is about a thirty-minute walk." The driver shrugged. "Up to you."

"Fuck." Abbie heard Hunter say under his breath. He turned to her. "Stay right here. I'm gonna run inside and check."

A massive gust of wind hit.

"Some of those outer bands are already making their presence heard," the driver remarked.

At this point, Abbie was seconds from either peeing herself or crying. She turned to Hunter. "Hurry." He looked at her for a moment making her heart did that weird flip thing again.

He placed his hand on her cheek. "I'll be right back."

She couldn't stop herself from leaning into his embrace.

Then he was gone. He was through the sliding glass doors and out of sight.

"So, first time in a hurricane?"

Abbie turned her glare to the driver. "You annoy me."

He shrugged. "I annoy a lot of people."

Abbie closed her eyes. How in the hell had she gotten herself into this mess? How was it she was halfway across the country, flew in a plane, was about to die, and her last few moments on earth were going to be with a pompous driver and Hunter fucking James.

"Rupert!"

The driver looked at her sideways. "Name's Doug, but you can call me Rupert if it'll make you feel better."

"No dumb-dumb. Rupert's my cat. If I die out here, who's gonna take care of him?" Her heart raced. People die in hurricanes. More than plane crashes, right? Oh god, she was for sure going to die.

"Who's watching the feline now?"

"My mom," she answered checking her pulse to see if she was already dead.

"There's your answer. If you die, I'm sure your mom will keep it."

Abbie darted her eyes to him. "Ever the optimist," she scoffed.

"Am I wrong?"

"Probably not. She'd make sure he got the nicest turtlenecks and sweaters."

The driver turned to her with his brows scrunched. "What?"

With a sigh she pulled out her phone shoving it in the driver's face. "He's a hairless cat. He needs warmth."

The driver recoiled. "What the fuck is that?"

"I just told you. It's a hairless cat."

"Kill it."

Abbie shoved the phone back in her pocket. "Why do men always say that? Just so you know when men take off their pants and there is a pair of nasty hairy balls looking back at us, we don't say *kill it*."

"That's your first problem. You're looking at the wrong pair of balls." The driver winked at her.

"What the hell is going on here?" Hunter growled pulling Abbie to his side. "Nobody is looking at anyone's balls."

"Is he the one that has nasty hairy balls?" The driver nodded his head toward Hunter.

"Probably." She shrugged. "But I don't have first-hand knowledge, thank god."

"Abbie," Hunter growled low in his throat. And for the first time since Hunter had walked back into her life, she saw something in his eyes that made her breath hitch.

They were crazed.

Possessive.

It was hot.

Abbie forced herself not to look down at her lady bits. *Calm down, girls. Holy crap.*

"Get back into the car, Abbie." Hunter pushed her toward the door. Deciding it was best not to poke the beast while they were waiting for their imminent death, she did as he asked. To her complete surprise though, when he climbed in after her, he pulled her to his side securing his arm around her.

She stared at him with her brow raised.

"Don't. Not right now." He tightened his hold.

Okay, that was weird. Actually, the last five minutes were weird.

"Flights grounded?" the driver asked.

Hunter grunted his answer.

"Told you."

The driver pulled away from the curb. "Rooms are slim pickings right now, but I think there might be some left in the hotel up the street."

Abbie felt Hunter take a deep breath followed by a loud sigh. "Thanks, man. I appreciate you waiting for us. The attendant said they grounded all flights thirty seconds after I bought the airfare."

"Sure, they did." The driver looked back at them.

Hunter laughed. A deep laugh which scared Abbie. Maybe he'd finally lost his mind? She knew she had about forty-five minutes to go until she reached that point herself, but maybe Hunter was seconds from snapping.

And she was first in the line of fire.

She gulped as he focused on her with an intensity that unnerved her.

"Oh, look. There's a gas station open. Do you want me to stop and see if you all can get some snacks to ride out the storm with?"

The moment was broken again. She cursed herself. Why was there another moment to begin with? Stupid Abbie. Stupid moments.

"Yeah, thanks man," Hunter said letting go of her.

That's when she looked at the driver. "What do you mean ride out the storm?"

"The Governor put a curfew on the state. In about forty minutes everyone's on lockdown so you might as well get some snacks until it's lifted."

"Lockdown, as in like a prison lockdown?"

"Kinda, but not really," Hunter answered. "I've lived through a hurricane or two. Let me run in and grab some supplies if there is any. I'll be right back." He glared at the driver. "Mine." With that, he raced out of the car.

"Mine what?" Abbie yelled after him before looking back at the driver. "Mine what?"

The driver threw his head back in a deep laugh. So deep it was like he couldn't breathe.

"Oh, for fuck's sake." Abbie huffed as she plopped herself into the back seat. "Everyone has lost their fucking mind and we're all about to die. What a perfect way to go."

That only made the driver laugh harder. So hard, in fact he was now wheezing.

"Everyone can fuck the fuck off."

The driver placed his hand on his stomach as he doubled over in laughter.

*Assholes.* All of them.

After a few minutes, Hunter was back with a bag. Curious to see what he grabbed she opened the bag. "This is all candy." Then her eyes spotted the small box of tea. A ball formed in her throat, if they weren't about to die, she would have kissed him.

*Blahh,* What the hell? No, it didn't matter if him getting her some tea was by far the sweetest thing anyone had ever done for her.

They were about to die.

"It's better than nothing." Hunter grunted as he narrowed his eyes at her.

"Do not give me that look, Hunter. I will add you to my list of throat punches."

"Aren't I already at the top?" He arched his brow.

"You are now."

The driver still in hysterics pulled out of the parking lot and started driving down the deserted road. After a few minutes they pulled into a hotel.

The moment they were stopped, Hunter tossed Doug his card. That's when Abbie looked at the rate and blanched. "Holy crap, are you serious? Three-hundred dollars?"

Doug winked at her. "Hey, premium pricing what can I say? Plus, isn't your boss paying for it?"

Oh yeah, how could she forget? "Hunter, leave a hundred-dollar tip."

He sent her a wicked smile. "One fifty?"

"Hell yeah!" Abbie did a little dance as she got out of the car. Then another gust of wind hit her bringing her back to reality.

Holy crap they were about to be in a hurricane. She'd never been in a hurricane before.

"Let's get inside and rent some rooms," Hunter suggested as he grabbed his card from the driver. "Thanks. I hope I never see you again."

Doug's smile brightened. "We'll see."

Hunter shook his head as he tossed his bag over his shoulder. "I hope not." He then grabbed Abbie's free hand and pulled her toward the hotel entrance.

When they made it inside Abbie looked around, it was quiet. An eerie quiet. She didn't like it. Then she heard the whistling of the wind from outside. She *really* didn't like that.

This was it.

This was her last moments before she died. She knew it.

Poor Rupert.

Hunter squeezed her hand once more before he dragged her up to the front desk. "Hi, I was wondering if you had any rooms available?" Hunter asked brightly at the lady working behind the counter.

When Abbie saw the woman's face fall, her heart plummeted.

"Umm, I can check."

Abbie glanced at Hunter. What if they didn't have anything? What if they were forced to go back outside? In a hurricane...

Abbie looked behind her. Doug was long gone.

Great.

Sweat broke out on the back of her neck. Freaking great.

As dread washed over her Hunter nudged her shoulder getting her attention before he pointed her in the direction of a pitcher of water on the other side of the lobby. "Babe, can you do me a favor and get me a glass?"

Her eyes widened. "Babe?"

"Please, Abbie." Hunter's eyes pierced into her.

Was he crazy? There was no way in hell he was looking at her *like* that.

"Please, Abs. I'll take care of this. Just get me some water. I'm dying here."

"I'm gonna spit in it," she huffed as she narrowed her eyes at him.

"Fine." He lightly pushed her toward the pitcher and for some unknown reason, she went. Clearly, the traumatic events of the last fifteen hours had caused her brain damage.

Stupid Hunter.

Stupid hurricane.

Stupid Bill.

"Stupid everything," she grumbled as she walked away. Then she remembered what Doug had said about there not being any water. This might be the last bit of water she would ever come across.

Decided fate had given it to her. She grabbed the two pitchers, poured the remainder of the one into the other and pulled out her shirt.

Turning away from the front desk she did her best to hide. "Mine now." She carefully placed the pitcher under her top.

Abbie let out an ear-piercing scream as someone tapped her on the shoulder causing her to spill the water all down her front.

"God damn it! Now I'm gonna die of dehydration," she snapped as she turned to annihilate whoever had caught her. That's when she saw Hunter holding his stomach as he laughed.

"What the hell were you doing, Abbie?"

"I was making sure I had water to *ride out the storm.*" She gave him the 'duhh' look as she pointed to her wet front. "Thanks for scaring me. Now, I'm screwed."

Hunter shook his head. "You're not screwed. Come on."

Abbie tried to brush off some of the excess water. "Wait, she found us rooms?" Abbie no longer cared she was soaking wet. They weren't going to have to go back into the storm. *Hell yes!*

"Yeah," Hunter answered. "We're on the fourth floor."

Abbie quickly glanced around her and spotted a tiny rug in front of a window. She walked over to it and pulled it to where she'd spill the water. She then covered the puddle and dusted off her hands. "Now, no one will know."

"Did you just hide the puddle with a rug?" Hunter stared at her in disbelief.

"You say hide. I say destroying evidence." She shrugged before grabbing her bag. "Are we both on the fourth floor?"

Hunter mumbled something as he motioned to the elevator.

"What?"

He turned back. "Yeah."

"I hope our rooms aren't next to each other. I bet you snore."

"Uh, huh."

Once inside the elevator, it quickly took them to their floor. When they stepped out, Abbie followed behind Hunter as he walked up to room '4121'.

"Are you taking this one?" Abbie asked.

"We both are." He turned to her.

"What?"

Hunter smirked. That same smirk that made her want to tackle him to the ground. Before she got the chance though, he ushered her inside with a little more force than necessary.

"Are you freaking kidding me? You better be joking, Hunter or I swear to the Universe—" She stopped the second she was in the room. Her mouth fell open.

"This was the only room they had," Hunter announced appearing from behind her. "It just so happens to only have one bed."

# CHAPTER FOURTEEN

"WHAT DO you mean there was only one room?" Abbie spun around toward Hunter. "Wait, fuck there being one room, what in the hell did you just say? One bed! One. Freaking. Bed?"

Hunter shrugged as he walked past her taking his bag to the bed. "That's what I said."

"Oh, no, no, no. Over my freaking dead body." Abbie snatched her bag that she'd dropped and headed toward the door.

"Where are you going?"

"To get another room. What does it look like dumb-dumb?"

Hunter ran after her. "There aren't any."

"Pshh, it's a hotel. They always say that shit." As she reached for the handle of the door Abbie found herself flying through the air before landing on the bed.

"Not this time," Hunter snapped. "Don't forget we're about thirty minutes until landfall."

Abbie squeezed her eyes tight. *Goddamn it! Damnit,*

*straight to hell.* She'd somehow forgotten about her impending death by hurricane.

When she opened her eyes, she saw Hunter crouched in front of her, his eyes hard. "Why do *you* have a tude?" she scoffed.

"Because you are trying my patience, Abbie."

"Excuse me?" Her brows shot to the ceiling. "I'm trying *your* patience? I should get a gold medal for all the shit I've had to put up since you walked back into my life."

"What patience? Abbie, I've lost track of the number of times you've tackled me to the ground."

Abbie crossed her arms over her chest. "You've deserved it every single time. And that says more about you than it does me. It's not my fault you're a weakling and my plump ass can take you down with ease."

Hunter's eyes darkened as his lips thinned.

*Oh shit.*

He stood pulling away from her. "Whatever. Go down there if you want, Abbie. I'm done with this. I wasn't lying. We're about to be hit by a Category One Hurricane, if not Category Two. I'm surprised they even had a room at all. If they didn't, we'd be out there." He opened the curtain in the room to prove his point.

When Abbie saw the trees bend in the wind along with the copious amount of rain, she swallowed.

"Beggars can't be choosers." Hunter scowled at her.

The gravity of the situation hit. This wasn't some joke Hunter was playing on her like he did when they were younger. No, this was serious *and* dangerous. "Do you think we're going to be okay?" her voice sounded small, even to her.

Hunter walked over to the bed to crouched in front of her. "I think so. We're in a solid structure. They have running water we can fill up the tub and sinks. We're safer in here than we are out there." He hitched his thumb behind him pointing to the window. "And I promise you this, Abigail Collins, I will protect you with my life, nothing will ever hurt you. Do you understand?"

She stared at him for a few seconds before she nodded. How could she not? Hunter's words pierced through every wall she'd ever built.

*Abigail Collins...*

As long as she'd known Hunter, he'd never used her full name.

The wind started to howl causing Abbie to shut her eyes tightly. It was all too much.

When Hunter squeezed her thigh, Abbie peeked through one eye only to see him stand and walk over to the bag he'd gotten from the gas station.

With his back turned, she studied him. She couldn't stop herself.

His muscles rippled under his business shirt. Since he'd pulled the sleeves up, she was able to take in the tan of his arms. She'd never admired arms before, but on Hunter they were hot.

He had thick, strong, arms. Forearms that had carried her multiple times now. She'd be lying if she didn't admit it left her in awe whenever he effortlessly moved her.

Then there were Hunter's hands.

The same hands that had pinned her arms above her head causing a rush through her body each time. No matter how hard she tried to deny it.

Her eyes fell closed as she pictured Hunter pinning her hands above her as he kissed along her neck and down her body.

*What the hell?*

Her eyes shot open. She shook her head trying to get rid of the images, but it was no use. As her eyes honed back in on Hunter's arms, she decided it was time to jump off the nearest cliff.

Hunter turned slightly giving her the most delicious view of his backside.

Was she drooling? Abbie could swear she was drooling.

*No. Bad, Abbie. Bad! This is Hunter James. Stop it. It's just been too long since you've had some bow-chicka-wow-wow. Calm your crazed lady bits, you lunatic. This is Hunter James for the love of all things!*

Yes, Hunter James... the same Hunter James that was now bent over going through his suitcase.

Her nipples pebbled.

Abbie looked down snapping her attention from his ass. That's when she saw those two traitorous devils poking out through her wet shirt. *Oh, for fuck's sake.*

She jumped to her feet and headed toward the bathroom. Once she threw some cold water on her face, she'd be fine.

Absolutely fine.

Hunter turned back to the bed when he heard the bathroom door shut. He let out a deep breath as his hand rubbed his eyes.

The situation they were in had fully set in. He put aside the fact they were about to be in a hurricane, but seeing the look in Abbie's eyes nearly unmanned him.

Being this close to her and *not* being able to comfort her the way he wanted was killing him.

Walking back to the bed, he kicked off his shoes before removing his tie. This was going to be a test of his strength.

Hunter's eyes moved to the bathroom. On the other side of that door was the woman that made his dick stand at attention the second she sassed him. The woman that he spent years cursing until he realized there was no use fighting it.

On the other side of that door, stood the only woman that would ever make him feel whole.

The front desk had offered him a pull-out bed, but he declined. There was absolutely no way in hell he was going to miss the opportunity to sleep with Abbie in his arms.

To feel her curves next to his body.

To finally know what it's like to have her in his arms.

*Holy shit,* he sounded like a loser even to himself.

Shaking his head, he grabbed the bag of peanuts he'd taken from the bag and tossed some of them in his mouth.

Fuck, he needed a chill pill.

The wind picked up outside causing him to look out the window. As he focused on the trees, the kiss he shared with Abbie all those years ago came rushing back.

The rain started pelting the window causing a wave of concern to wash over him. This wasn't his first hurricane, but this one looked bad.

Add in the fact he was now locked away alone with Abbie had his heart seconds from exploding. "Fuck!"

He tossed the peanuts on the nightstand just as the bathroom door open.

"Excuse me?"

Hunter snapped his head to her as his breath caught in his throat the moment he saw her.

*Holy shit.*

Abbie was absolutely breathtaking. She had wiped

away all the makeup she had on, and tossed her hair into a messy bun.

With her shirt still wet from the crazy moment she had downstairs he was able to take in her curves. The curves that haunted him since her little stunt from the first day in the conference room.

That purple polka-dotted bra had starred in all his fantasies since. That's why it was one of the first things he packed.

Hunter bit the inside of his cheek as his dick took notice.

He wanted her.

He wanted her bad.

Hunter's breath deepened the moment Abbie took a step toward him.

"Did you just curse at me?" She crossed her arms under her chest ready for a fight.

Hunter smiled at her ready to attack him stance. "No, I did not curse at you."

She sent him a glare. "Really? because it sounded like you did, bub."

Hunter's eyes shined, if Abbie wanted to fight, he was ready. However, this time there wasn't going to be any backing down. "While you were in the bathroom did you forget to take your angry pills?"

Abbie's eyes hardened as her breath came in short pants.

Maybe it was wrong of him, maybe he knew he shouldn't have done it, but he didn't give a shit. His lips formed into the smirk he *knew* would get her exactly where he wanted her.

In a split-second, Hunter was off the bed; his arms open ready for her lunge.

He was done playing this game.

The moment she was in his embrace, he wrapped her legs around his waist and pinned her against the nearest wall. He watched her face as she blinked a few times trying to register what he'd done.

"Abbie..." The air in the room thickened. This was it, he wasn't pulling back now. "Kiss me."

Her mouth fell open as she stopped fighting against his body. "What?"

As Hunter stared into her eyes, he knew it was time. Even if it killed him, he couldn't go another second without his lips on hers. "I dare you."

# CHAPTER FIFTEEN

*I* DARE YOU.

Abbie stared Hunter with her mouth wide open.

A dare.

What were they, ten?

*Damn it!* Her body reacted to him. Abbie tried to fight it. She tried to fight every instinct inside of her. She really did, but with the way his body pressed against hers, the heat that radiated off him sent shock waves through her that went straight to her core.

On top of that, her body had lost its goddamn mind. On their own, her hips started *grinding* into him.

Fucking grinding. Oh, god, she wanted to scream in frustration. *What the hell body?*

The moment she looked into his eyes, she lost it. To her utter dismay, Abbie let out a whimper. She'd never whimpered before in her life.

But with the intense lust-filled gaze staring back at her, it was enough to make all her logic fly out the window.

Hunter's body was making her do all sorts of things she'd never done.

Apparently, that included her fucking rubbing her pussy against Hunter's crotch.

As her hips involuntarily circled around his waist, she slammed her eyes shut the second she felt his dick.

*Effe, me.* He was big.

No, Hunter wasn't big, she pushed the thought away. It was her overactive imagination playing tricks on her.

He must have read her mind because he pushed his waist into her making Abbie feel his full length.

Well shit, this just got interesting.

A primal grunt escaped Hunter's lips causing Abbie to dart her eyes to his mouth.

Could she do this? Could she actually *kiss* Hunter?

She closed her eyes. The last time she kissed him, her whole world turned upside down. He broke a piece of her, and no matter how bad she wanted to taste him right now, she would never let herself feel that way again.

It didn't matter how bad her delusional body wanted him.

They weren't kids anymore.

Dares meant nothing to her.

A deep noise coming from his throat had Abbie's eyes snapping to his. They were hard, intense. They blazed with so much heat it was like the air had been sucked out of her lungs. "I *dare* you, Abbie."

Dare.

There was that word again. However, this time it flipped a switch inside of her.

*A Collins never surrendered.*

*A Collins never backed down.*

*A Collins never turned down a dare!*

Fuck it.

Abbie grabbed the sides of Hunter's face and slammed

her lips to his. It was probably the dumbest thing she had ever done, or would ever do, but right now she didn't care.

She was hungry for him and consequences be damned.

He kissed her back with such a possessive force, all rational thoughts flew out the window as she fought for control of their lips.

It was overwhelming.

He pulled her into his body, grinding his hips into hers as he dominated their embrace.

And, Abbie let him.

His kiss was desperate, and he was desperate for her.

As her hands roamed Hunter's body, she found herself yanked way from the wall before being *tossed* into the air. When she landed on the bed in a not so gentle bounce, she sent an evil look in his direction. "Hey! Watch yourself!"

However, Abbie's agitation flew right out the window the second Hunter pull his shirt over his head. With avid eyes, she watched his muscles move as he climbed onto the bed toward her.

God, his body was mesmerizing. No matter how bad she knew she should look away, she couldn't. His chest was delicious, sure she knew he had abs, she'd felt them the numerous times she'd tackled him to the ground, but seeing them in the flesh was something else.

*I wonder what they taste like?*

Wait a second. What the fuck was she thinking?

Then Hunter's hand skimmed along her leg as he crawled up her body.

*Oh god, oh god, oh god, she had to stop this. This was Hunter James.*

*Hunter. Fucking. James.*

The moment his hand reached her thigh, he squeezed

as he let out a deep growl. The sound went straight to her core, as Abbie's jaw dropped. *Holy shit, that was hot.*

"These thighs are gonna be *perfect* around my head." To emphasize his point, Hunter squeezed her thigh again causing a moan to escape Abbie's lips.

She struggled to regain any sense as Hunter pushed her thighs apart making room for his knees. She gulped. She'd never felt more exposed and she was still wearing all her clothes.

"Do you want that, Abbie? Do you want your legs wrapped around my head as I fuck you with my mouth?"

Did she? Hell fucking yes, she did. At this point, she'd be a fool to say no, and her mother didn't raise a fool. As heat spilled through her lower belly, she nodded.

"Good."

Abbie expected Hunter to pull off her pants but to her surprise, he bent kissing her stomach. His hands then went to her hips before pushing her blouse up exposing her soft rounded belly.

*Oh, no.*

Abbie's eyes slammed shut as she pulled down her shirt to cover herself. Before she knew it, the same hands that were trying to hide herself were now pinned effortlessly above her head as Hunter towered over her.

Without giving her a second to respond Abbie found his lips on hers again in a searing kiss.

Was his goal to make her lose her mind? 'Cause he was doing a damn good job of it if he was.

When Hunter pulled away, she opened her eyes only to see Hunter lifting her shirt higher.

"Fuck me, you're beautiful." His words sent a chill down her spine. They were spoken with such a possessiveness a new rush of heat went straight to her core.

"W-what?" she stammered, trying to find her voice.

Hunter's eyes snapped to her causing her breath to catch in her throat. His intense green eyes held such a primal need she no longer knew which way was up. No one, and she meant no one had ever stared at her that way before.

"I need to fuck you, Abbie," he got out through clenched teeth as his hand squeezed her hip in a move to clearly mark her. "I need to fuck you and hard. I've waited way too long for this."

As Abbie tried to make sense of his words, Hunter moved back down the bed positioning himself between her legs.

What was she to do? Because right now she wanted that too. As he reached for the waistband of her pants she lifted her hips giving him whatever he needed. He slowly pulled them down her legs. His fingers lightly skimmed her skin searing everywhere he touched.

"Fuck it!"

That's when Abbie heard the distinct sound of material being destroyed.

She looked down as her eye twitched. That asshole had ripped her pants and right now she only had one leg clothed. She pushed herself onto her elbows. "Are you kidding me?"

"I don't kid about sex, Abbie."

Her eyes narrowed as her lips formed into a thin line. "You fucking ripped my pants. I should stab you."

He sent her his signature smirk. "You can stab me *after* you come on my face."

Before she could argue though, Hunter was on his forearms with his face in her core. "Goddamn, Abbie, you're so wet I can see it through your panties."

Abbie's cheeks heated.

When his fingers lightly grazed her lower lips through the material she jumped off the bed.

"I've got to say, Abbie, ever since seeing your little duckies eating popcorn I've wondered what other fun surprises you had in store for me under your clothes."

Her eyes widened hearing his words.

*Damn it!* That's when she remembered what underwear she had on. *For fuck's sake.*

Deciding it was better to ignore it, Abbie fell back on the bed and looked up at the ceiling. *Universe, why do you continuously do this to me? Am I only here for your entertainment?*

"I've been dreaming about what I'd discover once I finally got you under me."

*Finally?* Wait, that made her sit up.

Hunter smirked at her once she caught his eye. "I'm happy to report I never thought tiny dinosaurs on skateboards giving the middle finger would make my dick so hard I'm about to come in my pants."

"You're about to what?" Abbie's eyes bulged.

Hunter sent her a playful wink. "Don't worry if I do, with the way you turn me on, *including* your insanely adorable panties I'll be hard again in seconds."

"Don't talk about my underthings."

"You mean these *underthings?*" Hunter trailed his fingers at the apex of her legs causing a hiss to escape her.

"It pains me to do this."

"Do wha—"

He grabbed the crotch of her underwear and ripped them off her body.

"My dinosaurs!" she yelled ready to attack. Her shock

was short-lived though, as her growl turned into a moan as Hunter's fingers touched her core.

Her completely naked core.

He lowered himself to his chest positioning his face at her center. "I knew you had a hairless pussy." He chuckled causing her to look down her body.

Bad choice.

Seeing Hunter between her legs had Abbie's head exploding. She didn't know whether it was the anticipation, or you know, the fact that it was Hunter James. The one person she was supposed to hate for eternity.

Then he winked at her.

Hunter lowered his head placing a gentle kiss to her mound.

Abbie tried to jump away from him but he was too fast. He shoved his hands under her legs before reaching around grabbing her hips.

"Fuck, Abbie, your pussy's so plump and juicy." He then kissed her mound again, but this time she felt his tongue.

"Oh, god, what are you doing?" she said in a panic. This wasn't happening. Nope. She somehow tripped coming out of the bathroom, fell and busted her head open and now was in some twisted coma induced hallucination.

*Holy mother of fuck.*

Hunter used his two fingers to pull apart her lips before raking his tongue on her clit.

"Something I've dreamt of doing for years." He sealed his mouth to her core.

"Oh, fuckity, fuck." Abbie closed her eyes as the sensation rocked through her. She was so close already, which was magic upon itself.

Then she felt a twinge of pain followed by a hoarse

growl. She promptly plopped herself onto her elbows glaring down at him. "Did you just bite me?"

"Yes. And I'll do it again." His eyes burned into her over her center. They were so intense, so possessive. So, fucking hot.

"Eyes on me the whole time, baby. You got that?"

She blinked at him. "What?"

When he lifted his head, she saw his chin glistening. Holy smokes, was that from her? Heat cascaded up her body as her heart felt like it was seconds from exploding in her chest.

"You heard me, Abbie." His growl sent another chill that went straight to her center. "Eyes on me the whole time. I want you to make no mistake. You're gonna know exactly who's eating you." It was if his hunter green eyes pierced into her soul.

What could she say to that?

Nothing.

Absolutely nothing.

It didn't matter. This was all a trauma-induced hallucination anyway. Why fight it? But she had to say, she would never be able to wipe her mind of who was between her legs. Hunter had officially burned this image into her brain.

She'd be sitting on a rocking chair fifty years from now and *still* remember who did this to her.

Stupid man.

Deciding it was best to deal with the repercussions of him ruining her later, she nodded.

Hunter must have believed her since he lowered himself back to her center. "Fuck, you taste good," he mumbled through her folds which sent another shock wave through her. His lips were so close to her clit, it was like a vibrator as he talked.

Abbie's stomach clenched as he sucked the bead into his mouth and hummed. "Oh god, no one, no one has ever..." She panted losing her words.

"No one has ever what?" he asked as he kept his mouth close to her clit while locking his eyes with hers.

It was too much. It was all too much; the sensation running through her body was enough to kill her. It was like every single nerve ending in her was on fire and there was no relief in sight.

This is how she was going to die.

Great, her tombstone was going to read something ridiculous like, *R.I.P Here lies Abbie Collins she died when her childhood nemesis decided to play fucking harmonica on her lady bits.*

Abbie held her eyes shut, as she tried everything she could to control her body. That's when she felt the pinch again.

He bit her.

Again.

Her eyes darted open as she stared at him, unable to form words as his fingers stroked her folds.

"Eyes on me," he demanded. "I won't tell you again."

A challenge, really? He should know better. "Or, what?"

Hunter lifted his head slightly. "Try me and you'll find out."

She swallowed.

"Now tell me, Abbie, no one has ever what?" His hand moved to her clit, which shot a new wave of pleasure through her. One she couldn't control no matter how hard she fought it.

"Come! No one has ever made me come like that!"

He increased his pressure causing her to finally tip over

the edge. Abbie shrieked as her orgasm hit her with the kind of power and force she'd never experienced before. Her whole body shot off the bed as he never let up on her clit causing her orgasm to consume every part of her.

After what felt like an eternity, and the last shock wave finally subsided. Abbie fell back onto the bed, her eyes closed tight.

*I'm dead.* This is what death felt like.

*Death by orgasm.* That's what her tombstone was now going to read.

Hunter moved causing the bed to dip, but honestly, she didn't have the strength to see where hallucination Hunter was going.

"That will be the first of many."

*That* gave her some energy.

Abbie opened one of her eyes and peered in his direction. "Many what?" she panted.

Once she finally thought she was no longer in danger of dying, she focused her attention back to Hunter. That's when she saw him move off the bed. *Wait, where was he going?*

This better not have been some joke. If he was about to walk out of this hotel room, he was a dead man.

Scratch that. He'd never make it two steps. Abbie pulled her legs up preparing to tackle him. Now that she had her taste of Hunter, this wasn't over.

Not by a long shot.

Once she got onto her knees. though, she stopped.

No, Hunter wasn't leaving. Far from it.

Instead, his hands were at his belt undoing it.

*Oh. Just kidding.* Abbie pulled down her shirt covering her stomach as she sat back on her ankles watching the show.

*Might as well commit this to memory, too.*

As he unzipped his pants, Abbie's breath caught at the sight of the top of his groin. "Oh my god, you aren't wearing any underwear!"

He smirked as he sent her a devilish wink. "I never do."

Abbie's mouth fell open. How the hell was she going to go on with the rest of her life knowing he never wore underwear.

How?

At this point, Hunter had destroyed her brain.

He then pushed his pants down to his ankles.

Her eyes widened as the *thing* bounced. As she tried to take him in, from his muscular thighs, his taut stomach, his Greek-god like features, her eyes kept being drawn back to the appendage between his legs.

The one that was staring at her.

The one that now terrified her. Sure, she was a curvy girl, and Abbie could handle a lot, but this... Holy fucking monster. "How in the hell do you walk around with that thing?"

"That's why I don't wear underwear," he laughed.

"Don't say shit like that, Hunter." She groaned.

"Why?"

"'Cause, I won't be able to forget it." She narrowed her eyes at him as that stupid smirk appeared on his face.

"Good."

Not good.

Not good at all.

Abbie's focused on the spot between his legs. At least that answered one question. If she ever saw Doug again, she could one hundred percent inform him Hunter did *not* have gross nasty balls.

On the contrary, the way he looked only made her want to do one thing... Crawl over to Hunter and take a taste.

"If you keep looking at me like you're dying of thirst and my dick is the only water you've seen in weeks, babe, I'm gonna nut."

That was hot. Her body quivered at his words. Really hot. A devilish smile spread across her face.

Hunter shook his head as a chuckle escaped him. "I knew it."

"Knew what?" Abbie quirked her brow at him.

"That you were absolutely fucking wild." Abbie had no time to react. He shot to the bed pushing her backwards. Before she knew it, her shirt was tossed across the room and both of her arms were pinned above her head.

*What the hell?*

Hunter hovered over Abbie as he drank her in. She was fucking beautiful.

Holy shit, it took every ounce of control he had not to lose it. And the sad thing was, she still had her fucking bra on.

Lord help him when he finally saw her tits. Even right now, they were spilling out of the top nearly giving him a heart attack. He'd always wondered what color her nipples were.

Did they have a light dusting of rose color? Were they pink? Maybe even a dark brown? A growl escaped him.

It didn't matter, because he was about to find out.

Sure, Abbie was pissed about destroying her other clothes but he didn't give a damn. There was only one thing standing between him getting his answer.

He grabbed the cups of her bra with both his hands.

"I'll murder you, Hunter James." Abbie's hands shot to his as she sent him a death glare. "You won't make it out of this room alive."

*Okay then.* He held his hands in surrender as he smirked. "Fine, but if you don't take it off in the next two seconds it's going the same way the dinosaurs did."

"And I'll make you eat your balls." She pushed at his chest making him fall back as she lifted herself . She took off her bra and tossed it on the floor. "There. See, was that so hard? Nothing was destroyed in the process."

"Pity." Hunter's eyes zoned in on her chest. *Fuck me,* he let out a deep groan. They were a perfect heavy teardrop shape that begged for him to explore.

His eyes moved to her nipples.

A light dusting of rose color. His dick jerked.

He'd never get the image out of his head. *Thank fuck.*

Instantly, Hunter was on her chest sucking the pert peak into his mouth.

Dear God, she tasted good. He could get used to this.

After a few moments, Hunter released her with a pop before giving the other one attention. The second Abbie arched her chest into his mouth with a moan he lost it.

He needed her. And now.

Hunter released her nipple and kissed his way down her body.

"Stop touching it," Abbie snapped.

His brow cocked as he looked up from her stomach. "What?"

That's when Abbie shimmied away from him before placing her hands on her belly. "Stop touching it, okay?"

"Touching what?" He sat back, watching her.

"My stomach."

Hunter stared at her in complete disbelief as a sadness entered her eyes.

Oh, hell no. Hell fucking no.

Out of nowhere, Abbie reached for a nearby pillow to hide herself.

*Fuck that.*

Hunter snatched the pillow from her grasp and tossed it forcefully through the air as his eyes narrowed dangerously at her. "What the hell do you think you're doing, Abbie?" In a split-second he had his legs pinned on either side of her waist as he held her arms down.

"Get off me!"

"No."

Abbie's eyes hardened. "Yes, you ogre. Get. Off. Me."

"No." He hovered over her. "Why the fuck did you just try and hide yourself from me?"

"I'm not."

He arched his brow.

"Whatever, Hunter. Get off, we're done here."

That pissed him off.

A lot.

They were far from done. And if he had any say in it, this was only the beginning.

"I didn't realize how much of a coward you became."

Abbie snapped her eyes to his. "Excuse me?"

"You heard me, Abbie. You've gone soft. The Abbie I knew would never hideaway."

"I'm not hiding, jack ass."

"That's what it looks like to me."

"Fuck you, Hunter."

"We're getting to that, but not until you understand one thing..." He didn't give her the chance to protest. Instead, Hunter captured her lips with his.

"You're mine, Abbie." He pulled away so he could look into her eyes. "*All* of you."

"I'm no ones." Her eyes hardened.

"You're wrong." He placed his fingers on her lips. "These lips. They're mine."

He moved to her chest. "Mine."

He then trailed his hands to her belly. When he felt her flinch under his touch, his teeth clenched. "This belly. The same belly that turns me on and I can't fucking wait to come all over. It's mine. Your curves... also mine. Understand this now, Abbie. There's no way in fucking hell I'm going to stop touching what's mine."

Abbie stared at him in shock. "Have you lost your mind?"

"When it comes to you, yes." Letting go of her abdomen, Hunter shimmied down her legs. "You need to understand this and understand it now, babe. I have waited long enough for you. *Every last inch of you.* It's about high time you figured that out."

Holy fuck what was wrong with him? He'd never in his life acted this insane when it came to sex. But when Abbie was involved, he couldn't think straight.

He moved his eyes back to hers.

Abbie got this wicked smile on her face as she wiggled under him. "You talk a lot of game there, Hunter. Mine this and mine that." Her eyes danced with amusement. "One orgasm does *not* make you king."

Oh, this was about to get fun. Apparently, Abbie no longer had any issues with her body. Instead, feisty, daring Abbie was back.

This he liked.

"How many does it take?" He asked before positioning himself at her center.

"More than you've got."

"Is that a challenge?" His brows shot to the ceiling.

"No. It's a dare."

Just like that, it was on.

Hunter pushed inside her causing Abbie to jump from the bed.

Feeling her walls tighten around him was almost more than he could handle.

Abbie started withering beneath him.

"Fuck, you feel good," he got out through clenched teeth.

"Harder," Abbie screamed as she pushed into his thrusts. "Fuck me like you mean it."

Oh, he was gonna fuck her all right. "Your wish is my command." Without giving her a second to think, Hunter grabbed her hips, pulling all the way out before flipping her over onto her stomach. He then pulled her hips up forcing her to keep her chest down.

Abbie swayed her ass in the air, causing Hunter's eyes to hone in on her center. Fuck her pussy beckoned him. It was full, ripe, juicy. He could see her glistening with her cream.

When he heard a small giggle, he looked from her ass to her face, that's when he saw her smiling from over her shoulder.

*Taunting* him.

He lost it.

Hunter's hand came down onto her ass, causing a loud smack to reverberate throughout the room.

"I'll kill you!" Abbie's eyes hardened, but she pushed herself back begging for more.

He trailed his fingers along her skin. "Can't hear you."

He used his right leg to push her knee causing Abbie to open further for him.

Fuck, the sight in front of him was a masterpiece.

Without thinking, Hunter leaned forward and took a quick swipe of her glistening folds with this tongue.

Shit, he could get used to this.

When he pulled away, Abbie pushed her hips back begging for more contact. Oh, he was going to give it to her, after all a dare, was a dare.

He positioned himself behind her before guiding his dick to her slit.

"What the hell is taking you so long?" She pushed her ass back causing him to slide fully inside of her.

Hunter's hands shot to her hips as her walls clenched around him. "Fuck."

"I'm trying!" She pushed back into him.

Hunter smacked her ass again with a laugh as he pulled out only to push back into her. "My dear, Abbie, I'm about to fuck you so hard, you'll never forget I was inside you." With that, Hunter pulled all the way out before slamming into her with such force the hotel bed shook.

Abbie's moan of pleasure only egged him on though. As he moved inside of her, Abbie met him thrust for thrust.

He squeezed her hips as he brought his dick all the way out as he looked down at their conjoined bodies. He was seconds from coming. Slowly, he pushed himself back inside her as he watched his dick disappear into her folds.

The sight aroused something inside of him. He almost couldn't believe it. After all these years he was *finally* inside of her.

*His* Abbie.

And there was no way he was ever letting her go.

"Harder, Hunter," she screamed. "Put your back into it. Use some of those stupid muscles of yours and fuck me."

He snapped. Abbie *always* knew how to get to him. And If she wanted harder, he'd give it to her. Hell, he would give her anything she wanted.

"Please," she begged as he withdrew slowly.

He smacked her ass and plunged inside of her.

Hunter leaned over her body placing his chest on her back as he thrust his hips. Abbie's panting under his made him snap. When his mouth came in contact with her shoulder, he bit down.

He couldn't help it.

That's when Abbie let out what he could only describe as a war-cry as she tightened around him. The feeling of her exploding around his dick did something to him.

It was like something he'd never felt before. Maybe it was the rawness of them, maybe it was his adrenaline. Fuck, maybe it was the storm blaring outside.

But as he felt her clench tighter around his dick, he knew exactly what it was. There was absolutely no denying it.

It was Abbie.

Hunter moved faster as she rocked back into him as she came. He lifted onto his knees as his hands went back to her hips holding her still.

As Abbie tightened around him one last time, he let out a primal grunt. One he'd never heard himself do before.

And as he coated her walls, for the very first time in his life, Hunter finally felt like he was home.

# CHAPTER SIXTEEN

Abbie's eyes shot open as a gust of wind hit the hotel room window. She blinked a few times trying to adjust her sight. Then out of nowhere, another gust of wind and rain pelted the window.

*The hurricane!*

How could she have forgotten?

*Oh god.* Her heart sank. She was in the middle of a hurricane, in a strange place, that she *flew* to...

When she felt something squeeze her waist, Abbie nearly jumped out of her skin.

Her eyes shifted from side to side as she realized not only was *something* wrapped around her, there was also something, a big something a really *hot* something, laying half on her.

Her heart pounded as she slowly turned her head toward it.

There was hair, very dark hair.

Abbie swallowed. Hair that could *only* belong to one person.

Ice ran through her body as everything came rushing back in an instant. *Oh, no, oh no, oh, no. I didn't.*

There was no way in hell she slept with Hunter.

*No.*

Images of her begging him to go harder pounded her brain. What was wrong with her?

This was worse than dying in a plane crash. This was way fucking worse.

Tears pooled in Abbie's eyes as she desperately tried to regain any sense of composure. It wasn't working.

Being as careful as humanly possible, Abbie took her left hand and slowly lifted the sheet. The gust of cold air hitting her body had her snapping down the material.

*Oh, for fuck's sake!*

She was naked, one hundred percent naked. As carefully as she could, Abbie lifted the sheet a few inches higher and looked again.

*Ahh!*

Abbie looked further under the sheet. *Damnit!* Hunter was naked too.

*You have got to be fucking kidding me!* She slammed her eyes shut. Sweat broke out on her forehead as her heart felt like it was seconds from jumping out of her chest. Images of them together bombarded her.

Hunter between her legs. Hunter ripping her clothes off. Hunter smacking her ass as she dared him to fuck her harder.

What the hell had she done?

She *dared* him. Dared. Oh, my god, she wanted to vomit. How could she have let her judgment slip that bad? Sure, she'd had some fantasies about Hunter, but that was in her mind. Not actually living them out.

Fuck.

And the way he savaged her body. She'd never had it that rough before...

She let out a groan.

She liked it.

She liked it a lot.

Her core tightened as she felt her nipples peak.

Abbie lifted the sheet again to send an evil glare at her body. *Knock it the fuck right off there, sisters. You are not getting excited over Hunter James. That stops right now.*

She turned her head to look at him. How had her life come to this?

Another gust of wind and rain hit the window which caused her to jump. *What fucking level of hell is this?* She narrowed her eyes at the ceiling. *You better hope I don't die today, Universe. 'Cause if I do, I'm going right up there and finding the first thing I can throat punch. You hear me?*

A tree branch hitting the window caused Abbie's eyes to widen.

*Kidding.* She held her hands in surrender. *I was only kidding. Okay, I'm not, but I hear you. Don't piss off the angry Universe.*

Abbie closed her eyes praying for death.

Then Hunter grunted from next to her reminding her who was there.

How in the ever-loving hell was she going to get out of this mess? Opening her eyes, she looked to the ceiling once more. *Universe, hey, you, it's me, Abbie again. You know the one that just threatened to punch you. I was totally joking. See, haha. I'm such a kidder. I mean seriously, me, throat punch you? Haha. Yeah, well anyway, umm, if you'd be so kind as to get me out of this situation, I'd gladly give you five dollars this time. That's four more dollars than last time.*

Abbie waited a few seconds.

*Anytime this century would be nice.*

Then to her complete surprise, Hunter released her waist before turning to his back.

*Holy fuck! Screw the five dollars, I'm giving you twenty! Thank you, thank you, thank you!* Abbie wanted to cry at her new-found glimmer of hope.

As quietly as she could, Abbie pushed herself onto her elbows. As she looked over Hunter's body and got her first sight at the window.

Holy crap it looked bad. Really bad. The trees outside looked like they were about to snap, while the rain formed a white curtain over everything.

She gulped.

Maybe if she didn't look outside it would get better. Slowly Abbie's eyes then moved to the man sleeping soundly next to her.

Abbie cocked her head to the side. How in the world was he sleeping through this?

*Oh yeah*, she smacked her forehead with her hand. He was probably exhausted. You know that happens after you nearly rip someone in two with your dick. Ugh.

Abbie closed her eyes. Yep, she had sex with her childhood nemesis.

Wonderful.

Fucking wonderful.

Now, what the hell was she going to do about it? She looked around.

Bathroom.

Get to the bathroom.

Clean up. Then figure out how to get the hell away from Hunter.

Her stomach bottomed out at the gravity of the situation. Holy shit if she decided to stay with WCM this was going to be an HR fucking nightmare. Martha would have a field day. She wanted to scream.

Thank god the light in the corner of the room was still on.

Abbie took one deep breath before she carefully — like defusing a bomb carefully, pushed the sheet off of her body.

Once it was off, she had to stop herself from groaning. *That's right dumb-dumb, all your naked bits are flapping around.* She rolled her eyes as she let out an annoyed groan. *I'm so mad at you right now, body! Couldn't you have kept your legs closed? One promise of an orgasm and poof you open like a hot summer day and the dick was a popsicle.*

Deciding it was best to forget it ever happened, she placed both her hands behind her and pushed her butt into the air, scooting it over to the edge of the bed.

She looked back at Hunter. Seeing he hadn't moved she turned and put her left foot on the floor.

One foot down. One to go.

However, right as Abbie lifted her other leg, she heard a grunt causing her to turn toward Hunter. *Shut up! This is all your fault anyway!* Her gaze scanned down his back since it was now uncovered and stopped on his ass.

A growl escaped her as she sent it a scowl. Why did it have to be so firm and touchable? Stupid butt.

After a few more seconds and no noise from Hunter she figured she was in the clear.

Abbie carefully placed her other foot on the ground. As soon as it hit the floor, she felt like she'd won a million bucks.

*See, you are a master at this, Abbie. It's like you're a ninja. Maybe that should be your new career of choice.*

*Abbie Collins, Master Ninja.* Lord knew she'd never be able to show her face again in Advertising.

*Okay on the count of three, stand up. You've got this. If Hunter hasn't woken while it's World War Three outside, then standing up won't do it.* She looked back at him one more time to make sure he was indeed asleep. He was. Okay...

*One.... Two.... Three.*

She stood.

*Success!*

In her complete excitement of her ninja skills, Abbie hadn't paid attention to what she was doing. As she took a step forward her left knee slammed into the nightstand causing it to rumble.

Abbie threw her hand over her mouth holding in the scream as the pain ricocheted through her body.

*Mother fucker. Son of a bitch. Are you fucking kidding me right now?* She squeezed her eyes shut cursing her stupidity.

Once the pain subsided, she froze listening for any sign of Hunter.

After a few moments of silence, she turned around to see him still fast asleep.

*What the hell? Is he dead? He has to be dead. Should I poke him?*

Abbie smacked her palm to her forehead. *What the hell are you thinking, dumb-dumb, should you poke him? What in the hell is wrong with you? You're trying not to wake him up. Seriously, Abs, sometimes I wonder about you.*

She rolled her eyes. *Great, now you're talking about yourself to yourself. Just how pathetic is this going to get?*

Abbie shook the thoughts from her head, she could deal with them once she was safely away from the biggest mistake of her life.

Taking one small step she tip-toed to the bathroom.

After realizing the coast was clear and Hunter at this point was probably dead, she ran.

The second she got inside the bathroom, she spun to see if she'd woken him.

Nothing. Seriously?

If she ever made it through this, Abbie was going to have to send him a telegraph to let him know he needed his sleeping checked. No one should sleep that soundly, especially in the middle of a dang hurricane.

Abbie nodded, proud of herself. See, she could still be concerned for someone else's well-being. Yep. It was decided as soon as she made it back home, she was sending him a note.

There was absolutely no way in hell she'd ever see him again. So, note in the mail it was.

Harnessing all her newly found ninja skills Abbie carefully shut the bathroom door.

Okay, it might have been the fact the rain was hitting the window hard, or that Hunter apparently slept like the dead, but Abbie wanted to believe in her bomb ass ninja skills.

Once she was safely inside, she finally took a deep breath. Abbie didn't dare turn on the light. At this point, it would be her luck the light would cause Hunter to finally wake up.

As she leaned against the door, tears formed in her eyes. How in the world was she ever going to survive this? How had her life turned into such a fucking mess? How could she had been so stupid to sleep with Hunter?

Hunter fucking James.

How?

And no matter how hard she fought against her mind, she liked it. She liked every dirty second of it.

Abbie pushed herself off the door and walked to the sink. She braced herself on the countertop with her hands as her head hung low with the gravity of the situation.

There were so many things she needed to sort out, but she had no idea where to start. From his words to his actions, to the fact he seemed to love her body. All of it.

One of her hands went to her stomach. She'd never had qualms about the way she looked before. Hell, if people didn't like her, that was their problem, not hers. But with Hunter, it was different.

Different was what they did.

It was always a competition with him.

Abbie closed her eyes as the memory of Hunter's touch on her skin filled her mind. He seemed to like it, wait no, he seemed to be possessed by it.

A shiver ran down her body as her gut twisted into knots. There was no way she was going to survive this.

Abbie placed her hand back on the sink as tears pricked her eyes. Life wasn't supposed to turn out like this. Nowhere in the cards, did she think Hunter would show back up or that she would end up sleeping with him.

It didn't make any sense, she was supposed to hate him.

Her heart constricted. But if she was supposed to hate him, why did she feel more at peace when he was there? And on the plane... She shook her head. Abbie wouldn't have survived if it wasn't for him.

A single tear fell from her eyes. With everything that happened, how was it possible that right now even though she hated Hunter, all she wanted to do was crawl back in bed with him.

What was wrong with her? Quickly, she wiped away the tears trying her best to control her heart.

For the first time since sneaking into the bathroom,

Abbie slowly looked up to stare into the mirror. She gasped in horror.

She was a mess.

A *freaking* mess. Her hair was all over the place, her face was puffy, and as she looked carefully down her body, she could already see bruises forming on her hips.

She groaned as she felt her world shattering around her. *Universe, it's me, Abbie, again. I know we've been having a crap ton of these heart to hearts. I'd like to say I'd tone them down, but who am I kidding? Is there any way—*

She froze mid-thought as a cold sweat broke out over her body. "We didn't use protection."

# CHAPTER SEVENTEEN

HUNTER STRETCHED as he slowly opened his eyes. Damn, he felt good. He didn't think he'd ever slept so well before.

He wasn't that surprised, though. Abbie was a fucking animal. After they finished, she passed out, and he was seconds from doing the same. He pulled the sheets over them and curled up with Abbie *finally* in his arms.

So, hell yeah, he slept great.

The sound of rain hitting the window reminded him of the hurricane. How had he forgotten? Moving his eyes to the window he watched the trees bend in the wind as the rain coated everything.

It was bad.

Really bad.

Hunter looked at the clock on the nightstand. They'd only slept for a few hours. Thankfully, there was still power.

His eyes shot to the window as a branch hit it. This had to be the winds at the eyewall. He'd been in enough hurricanes to tell. The eyewall was always the worst.

Then it went calm.

An eerie calm.

Even though everything became a standstill, the eye was by far the most dangerous. As the hurricane moved over you, the eye never lasted long. And what was on the other side was deadly.

Very deadly.

As the winds flipped directions, the danger only worsened.

Thank fuck the hotel had a room for them. If they hadn't found shelter who knows what could have happened.

But none of that mattered. They were safe.

And more importantly, Abbie - a *naked* Abbie, was lying right next to him.

His signature smirk appeared on his face as Hunter quietly stretched trying not to wake her, feeling his muscles loosen. Damn, he felt amazing. Finally, being able to touch, taste, *fuck* Abbie was a dream come true.

*His* dream come true.

The way she moved her body against his begging for more was caveman inducing.

Shit, Abbie was a fucking beast in bed.

Hunter's smirk turned into a full-on toothy grin as he realized with the way the hurricane was raging on outside, he figured they could get in a few more rounds before they got the all-clear.

The more he thought about it, the more he liked the idea.

Plus, with the way the sheet was now tenting at his lower half, he knew there was only one way to ease the ache in his groin.

*I've always wanted to wake someone up by my tongue being between their legs. Who better to do that with than Abs?* His mouth watered at the thought of her taste.

Fuck hurricane food, he knew *exactly* what he was having for a snack.

Hunter slowly – trying his best not to wake Abbie, turned his body to finally face her.

Everything stopped.

It was like a pocket of ice hit him. The sheets were empty.

As in fucking *empty*.

Dread washed through him as his eyes shot around the room.

Nothing.

Hunter's adrenaline kicked in as he jumped from the bed. He ran to the bathroom. When he pushed open the door only to be greeted with an empty room, his gut clenched.

Abbie was gone.

Panic ran through him. Holy shit she was fucking gone.

This couldn't be happening.

As he scanned the room, he noticed Abbie's suitcase still on the ground. *Okay, that was a good sign, right? I mean she didn't just up and leave and never plan to come back.* Her things were here.

And knowing Abbie, she wasn't walking around the hotel naked.

As fast as he could, he ran to his bag before throwing on a shirt and a pair of gym shorts. When he reached for his thing, he saw Abbie's phone on the floor.

A new wave of dread ran through him. She wouldn't have left without her phone, right?

His eyes moved to the window, as his heart slammed against his chest. The winds were dying down. That only meant one thing.

The eye was here.

Fuck. He had to find her.

Hunter quickly threw on his shoes as he ran down the hall, scanning his surroundings as he went. It was quiet.

Too quiet.

Deciding it was best to start in the lobby, he jogged to the elevator and hit the button. That's when the power flickered.

Once.

Twice.

Boom.

He was thrust into darkness. "Fuck, are you kidding me?" How could this get any worse? He groaned.

Hunter pulled out his cell phone. Turning on the in-camera flashlight he scanned his surrounding area. That's when he found the door to the staircase.

When he swung it open, he was surprised to see auxiliary lights. *Thank god, they must have a generator.*

As fast as he could he ran down the four flights of stairs until he reached the first floor. The moment he opened the door, he scanned the area.

Just like on the fourth floor there wasn't a soul in sight. Apparently, everyone else had the right idea by *staying* in their room where it was safe.

Hunter's eyes hardened. As soon as he got his hands on Abbie, he was going to kill her.

At least it was brighter down here. Since the lobby was full of windows, Hunter threw his phone back into his pocket as he headed toward the front desk. He wasn't the least bit surprised when he saw no one there.

Figures.

As he continued his search for Abbie, he ran into an employee. *Thank fuck.* At least there was another person around. Quickly Hunter jogged up to him. "Hey man, have you seen a woman about this tall, drop-dead curves, chestnut hair? Probably a little crazed, anywhere?"

The man arched his brow. "She like to mumble obscenities and threats to throat punch a lot?"

Relief ran through him. "That would be her. So, you saw her?"

"Yeah, I saw her about five minutes ago. She wanted to head outside." He shook his head. "She was kind of feisty."

His heart stopped. "What did you just say?"

"That she was feisty, well maybe angry I'm not really sure." The employee shook his head. "Maybe she was drunk? Either way, it was best to stay clear."

"You said she wanted to head *outside*?" Hunter's heart plummeted as the thought of Abbie going out into the hurricane ran through him. Why in the hell would she do that?

"Yeah," the guy answered with a shrug. "I told her she shouldn't and needed to get back up into her room. She then flipped me off, told me to shove it where the sun doesn't shine, before pointing outside saying it was clear."

"It's the fucking eye! It's not clear." Hunter's heart slammed against his chest with such force he thought he might have a heart attack.

"No need to yell at me. I *know* it's the eye. I tried to tell her that, but she was hell-bent on going out there."

"So, you let her leave?" Hunter's fists clenched. He could punch him and no one would know. The police couldn't come out in this storm even if they wanted to.

"I don't think you *let* that woman do anything. She does what she wants." He laughed.

"Does a statewide curfew mean nothing to you?" That's it, this guy was dead.

"Hey, I'm not the one headed out there, she was. You can't force someone to do something they don't wanna do.

That's not how the world works. I told her it was dangerous but she was dead set on going out there. I wasn't going to stop her and risk my life if she wanted to be stupid."

Hunter saw red, but he couldn't blame the guy. He was right, it wasn't safe and he knew Abbie. Keeping her against her will would *not* have ended well. "What store?"

"She asked where the nearest pharmacy was. I told her about four blocks away but I doubted they'd be open." He shook his head. "I don't think she heard that part. As soon as I told her which way she was out the door." The man looked at Hunter with concern. "She looked determined to get to the store. Is she okay?"

"If she is, she won't be when I get my hands on her." He glared out the windows. He was going to murder her. First, he was going to kiss her, but then he was going to kill her.

This was his worst nightmare come to life. Abbie was out there in the storm. In the eye of a fucking hurricane.

Yeah, if she was safe, she wouldn't be for long.

Hunter looked harder out the window, he could see the clouds moving as the rain started to pick back up.

This was dangerous.

He had to find her.

"Which way did she go?" he asked looking at the employee.

"That way." He pointed out the door and to the right.

"Thanks." Hunter ran out of the hotel and in the direction the guy mentioned.

Once he was outside, he looked to the sky, the clouds were moving faster, this wasn't good. If he didn't find her in time before the other side of the eyewall came, they were both screwed.

Abbie might be the love of his fucking life, but he couldn't love her if she was dead.

This was the stupidest thing she'd ever done. Even more stupid than all the dares they'd done before.

This took the cake.

As Hunter ran down the street, the rain increased causing his heart to slam harder against his chest.

What if he couldn't find her?

His eyes scanned every area as he searched. "Who the fuck goes out into a hurricane?" he growled as the rain pelted his face. "When I get my hands on you, Abigail Collins, you won't sit for a fucking week. No, make that a month!"

*Jesus fucking Christ.*

Not seeing her anywhere Hunter took the next right. As soon as he rounded the corner, he saw a curvy woman banging on a door.

He stopped as his heart jumped recognizing her. He'd never felt relief like this before.

*Stupid fucking woman.*

As he watched her bang on the door he took off. "What the hell do you think you're doing?" he shouted through the rain.

Abbie let out a high-pitched scream causing him to jump back. Her hand went to her heart. "Don't scream at me like that, assface."

His eyes dangerously hardened on her. "Abbie, you're out in a fucking hurricane. I will scream at you until I'm blue in the fucking face. I think I've had ten heart attacks by now."

When Abbie turned toward him, he saw terror in her eyes. "It's only a little rain, Hunter." She turned away from him in desperation before she started banging on the pharmacy door. "Please open up, you don't understand I *have* to get in there."

Hunter watched her in amazement.

"Please! I can't do this alone! I only have a few hours to take it. Please, please I'm begging you, please open up." Abbie fell to her knees as she pounded on the door. Hunter could swear he even heard a choked sob.

What the hell was so important she risked her life for? Shaking his head, Hunter looked around. The sky was getting darker. It was time to go. She could get whatever she needed later.

Screw this. Hunter took a few steps to Abbie before hoisting her into the air tossing her over his shoulder.

"What the hell, you Neanderthal. Let me down right now. I have to get inside."

"It's the middle of a fucking Hurricane, Abbie. No one is inside."

"They have to be. You don't understand. I'm not ready for this."

Just then a gust of wind hit them. That's it. They had to go. Hunter started running toward the hotel.

"I should fucking chain you to the bed for this stunt, Abbie," he shouted keeping his hand on her ass.

"What did you say?"

"You heard me, Abbie. This isn't a game." He was done. With Abbie on his shoulder he sprinted toward the hotel.

"No, Hunter you've gotta stop." Abbie pounded on his back. "You have to let me down right now. I *need* to get into the pharmacy. Right fucking now!" He heard the plea in her voice but he didn't care.

His only concern was getting them to safety.

As if on cue, the wind increased as the rain picked up. Hunter glanced around only to see the trees start moving in the opposite direction that they had before.

*Fuck!*

That meant the eyewall was here. The absolute worst part of the storm was about to be on top of them and they were still a few blocks from the hotel.

If they made it out of this alive, he was going to strangle her. Fuck her senseless first, and then murder her.

"You don't get it, Hunter, I have to get in there. Bring me back," she yelled into his back.

"Shut up, Abbie." Hunter slapped her ass as he continued running.

"Stop doing that!"

"No. When you finally act like an adult, I'll stop treating you like a child. Until then, when you act like a spoiled brat, I'm gonna smack your ass."

As the rain increased more Hunter prayed they'd make it before things started flying.

If you touch my ass one more time it will be the last thing you ever do!"

A gust of wind hit them causing Hunter to lose his footing. Once he steadied himself he looked up to see the hotel. *Thank god!*

"We didn't use anything!"

Hunter couldn't hear Abbie over the wind but he didn't care. She could continue to scream at him once they were inside the hotel.

"We need to go back to the pharmacy. We didn't use any protection!"

Anger coursed through him as Abbie's muffled words pissed him off. Didn't she get the fact she could die if they didn't get inside? She could bitch at him later.

As the wind picked up, he ran faster. It was only a few more feet to the door. Once his hand touched the handle instant relief swept through him.

They were going to be okay.

Hunter's breathing was heavy as he walked them further into the lobby. Once he knew they were somewhat out of harm's way he grabbed Abbie's hips taking her off his shoulder.

The second her feet hit the ground, she lunged at him. "I'm not on the fucking pill and you came in me!"

# CHAPTER EIGHTEEN

"Oh, for fuck's sake!"

Abbie collided with Hunter before she pinned him to the ground.

"Do you really have to do this every time something happens?" Hunter groaned as she landed on top of him.

His hands went to her hips as Abbie's eyes narrowed. Fuck this asshole. She was pissed for so many freaking reasons. How dare he carry her like a child on his shoulder? She was soaking wet, she was scared, and the most important thing...

He fucking came in her!

*Mother fucker.*

Abbie locked her legs around his waist. This was his fault. All of it. Every last fucking bit of it. If Hunter hadn't waltzed back into her life none of this shit would be happening right now.

"I hate you," she said in a menacing tone.

Hunter's face changed instantly.

Before she knew it, she was flipped onto the floor with Hunter staring down at her.

"No, you don't." His eyes were hard as he glared at her. How dare he?

"Yes, I do."

"No, you don't, Abbie."

"You don't get to tell me how I feel, Hunter. That's not how feelings work." She tried pulling out of his grasp but failed miserably.

"Yes, I do."

Abbie stopped fighting as she stared at him blankly. "I'm going to throat punch you."

"You know, Abs, you say that a lot, but you never follow through. I'm beginning to think you're nothing but talk. Talk is cheap, sweet cheeks." He stood before grabbing her hand pulling her onto her feet. "It's cold. I'm wet. You're wet. And it's not safe to be close to the door."

"What did you just call me?"

Hunter smirked at her. "Sweet cheeks."

"Why I ought to—" She never finished her sentenced. Hunter lifted her back into the air throwing her onto his shoulder. At this point she was beginning to think he was part caveman. "Stop manhandling me!"

"I'm about to manhandle you," he answered before smacking her ass.

Abbie was about to unleash holy hell on him, but her eyes caught sight of the window. Everything stopped for her.

It was terrifying.

The wind was ripping around the trees with so much force they looked as if they would snap in two. And the rain, it was like a monsoon.

Her face paled. She was outside in that. If Hunter hadn't come along she'd be trapped, or worse injured. Something flew across her view causing a chill to run down her spine.

That was really stupid.

What if something had hit her?

"It looks like you found her," a voice echoed throughout the area. "I'm glad I was a little worried there. This storm is no joke."

Abbie felt Hunter's hand rest on her butt. She might realize how stupid she'd been, but if he didn't remove his hand at once she was going to pulverize him.

"Yeah, I found her," he grunted. "I'm lucky I got her back before the eyewall fully hit."

"You are," the worker said. "People always think they can out smart a storm. You can't outsmart mother nature. That's why they call her mother. A mother always wins."

Abbie looked over her shoulder and cringed. Of course, it was the same guy she'd threatened and wished bodily harm against. Ehh, screw it. She sent him an evil glare too.

"We've got our backup generators going, now," he said cocking his head to the side as he looked at her. "Some lights will work but most won't. Your room doors will still open."

"That's good to know. Thanks." Hunter nodded.

"Anytime." The man smiled. "Oh, and just so you know there is an emergency kit with candles and flashlights in the hotel's closets." He shrugged "Hurricanes. Always gotta be prepared."

"Yeah," Hunter answered before hiking Abbie higher onto his shoulder. "Thanks again."

Before Abbie knew it, Hunter was in the stairwell taking the steps two at a time. *That was kinda hot.* The moment she caught herself, though, she groaned. *Stop it. None of that, stupid body. Haven't you done enough? This caused your problems in the first place.*

"Stop squirming." Hunter slapped her ass causing her to jump.

"Stop that. Put me down, ass-hat. Right now." She punched his back.

"No."

Abbie was getting really tired of his one-word answers. If she could, she'd take that one word and shove it right up his ass. "What do you mean, no?"

"Exactly that." He smacked her ass again before coming to the landing. He then swung open the door.

"Damn, I was hoping there would be some lights in the hall." Abbie felt Hunter rifling through his pockets. That's when he pulled out his phone. With the flashlight they were able to get to their room.

Although, the fact he still hadn't put her down pissed her off.

Hunter pushed open their door and walked inside. He tossed her onto the bed causing her to bounce.

"Hey, what the hell!" First, she was soaking wet, and second, screw him.

"Shut up, Abbie."

That made her send him a pointed look. "Don't you dare tell me to shut up."

Hunter's face was hard as he stared at her, his lips thin. "Do you understand how stupid you've been?"

Abbie opened her mouth but Hunter held his hand up. "No, your time for talking is done. You went out in a hurricane, Abbie. A *fucking* hurricane."

"I thought it was over, okay! It was barely raining and there was no wind."

"It was the fucking eye."

"I know that now! Stop yelling at me, okay?" God, why couldn't things with Hunter ever be easy? It was like the moment he came around all hell broke loose. Plus, this fucker had *yet* to acknowledge what she'd said.

That pissed her off. It was like he pushed right passed it. She was here to set him straight. He fucking came in her with no protection. *She* was being the responsible adult here and try to do something about it.

With the way he acted right now, he couldn't care less if she got pregnant. Well too bad for him, 'cause there was no way in hell she was tying herself to him.

When she finally looked at Hunter, he scowled at her.

"Why are *you* so angry? Okay, I get it. I fully admit I shouldn't have gone outside. You were right, but I had a good reason. I was trying to save us both from having a miserable life tied to—"

Hunter took two steps toward her before lifting her into the air.

"Put me down!"

Completely ignoring her, Hunter brought her into the bathroom only stopping at the closet on the way to grab a flashlight. "I'm angry 'cause you willingly put yourself in danger. I'm angry because I didn't know where you were. I'm angry because when I turned over in bed you were fucking gone. Gone, Abbie. I had no idea what happened." He smacked her in the ass once more. Hard.

Ignoring everything he said, Abbie pounded on his back trying to make him put her down. "What the fuck is wrong with you?"

"I like you better when you're not talking," he growled. "Or better yet when you have something in your mouth."

She gasped. How dare he? He wasn't going to have to worry about being a father, because she was going to strangle him.

He turned on the flashlight before placing it on the sink vanity.

As he lowered Abbie to the floor he didn't give her any time to react. Instead, he was pulling her wet shirt over her head before tossing it behind him.

"Hey!"

He silenced her with his lips.

This wasn't a kiss like earlier. No. This was filled with anger and desperation. This kiss consumed her.

And no matter how hard she tried to fight it, she couldn't. She leaned into him as his mouth explored.

Then before Abbie knew it, he was completely undressing her. First went her bra, followed by her pants, panties leaving her completely naked and dazed.

How in the heck?

Hunter stood back from her as she blinked a few times.

Did he just set a world record? If he didn't, he was damn close to it. Then she looked at him. Hold on, he was still fully clothed. "Hey, wait a minute, why am I the only one naked?"

She didn't have to wait for an answer, before the last word was out of her mouth Hunter was pulling his shirt over his head and removing his shorts.

Her breath caught in her throat. It was like the second he took off his clothes her dumb-dumb switch turned on and all logical thought left her brain.

Even through the dim glow of the flashlight, Hunter's body was a masterpiece. She'd never admit to that, but it was hard to look away.

He took a step closer to her before pulling her body to his. With a deep growl, he brought his lips to hers in a searing kiss.

She cursed herself as her body responded to him,

sending fire through every nerve ending she had. How did he always do this to her?

Then she felt him walk her backward to the tub before reaching behind them turning on the shower.

She pulled her lips from his. "Oh, heck no. We are not getting into there. Angry sex be damned. I'm not stupid enough to get in there during a hurricane."

"Oh," he groaned. "*Now,* you're concerned for your safety. Where was that thirty minutes ago?"

"Fuck you."

"I'm trying."

Her lips thinned. "I'm not getting into a shower while it's storming."

"For fuck's sake Abbie, get in the fucking shower. The rain wasn't warm."

As his words hit her, it was like the cold finally sank in. Her body prickled as she realized just how cold she really was.

"Get in."

"Stop bossing me around, Hunter." She poked his chest.

"Fuck it." He picked her up before placing her into the shower.

"Stop manhandling me, Hunter. I'm serious."

"Get this straight, Abbie, I *will* boss you around. Especially, when you're acting like a child."

Her mouth fell open.

"Second, like I told you earlier, *this* isn't manhandling, what I'm about to do to you is manhandling."

"You're such a pig."

"Sexy," he corrected. "And, you talk too much."

Before she could respond, his lips were on hers.

# CHAPTER NINETEEN

*Fuck!* Abbie talked too much.

And right now, it was time for anything but talking. After the insane events, Hunter needed to feel her body close to his. That was all he cared about.

Their kiss consumed him.

He was desperate, needy, and he wanted more. He wanted all of it. Her body, her mind, anything she would give him, and he was going to get it. The fact she could have been hurt changed everything.

As Hunter's hands trailed down her smooth curves, he stopped at her ass giving it a squeeze before pulling her the impossible inch closer.

However, to him, she still wasn't close enough. Abbie could have died out there.

He wanted to be inside of her. No, he needed to be inside of her.

"Hunter," Abbie panted as she pulled her lips from his.

He ignored her as he kissed along her jawline before bringing his lips to her again. They called to him, and he was done fighting.

Then her words from the lobby hit him. *She's not on the pill.*

Was it wrong his body reacted to that? He never really thought about having kids before. Maybe it was the fact his mom and dad had split when he was younger or what happened with his stepmom, but kids weren't in the cards for him.

At least they weren't with anyone but Abbie.

It was as if his body knew that before he did. And the thought of her belly growing with the child they created together did something to him.

The possessiveness he'd felt came rushing back in full force. Quickly he moved his hands to her ass palming them as he lifted her. Abbie wrapped her legs around his waist. Fuck she felt good in his arms. Backing her up, he pushed her to the wall before grinding his hips into her core.

Her heat was enough to make him explode right there and then. "Oh god," he groaned against her as she started circling her body desperate for friction.

"Please," she begged.

Hunter moved his hands to her ass cheeks before pulling them both off the wall. "Are you going to put yourself in danger again?"

Abbie looked at him confused. After a second of silence, he smacked her.

"Hey!"

"Answer me, are you ever going to be that stupid again?" He grabbed both of her cheeks grinding her lower half to his.

"I-I can't think when you do that."

"Do what? This?" He pushed them back to the wall before pulling a few inches away. He then lined his member to her entrance, enticing a hiss from her.

He pushed inside of her before he brought his head to her neck. That's when he bit her collarbone making Abbie dig her nails into his back.

"Hunter!"

He pumped inside of her, once, twice, and then pulled out. "Are you going to put yourself in danger anymore?"

"I can't make those promises," she panted "Since I don't know who's gonna piss me off tomorrow, but if you don't stick that thing back inside of me, *you'll* be in danger."

"Not good enough." He pushed inside her core before pulling out.

"Yes, yes I promise to do my best." That was all he needed to hear.

Hunter pulled Abbie's body to his as he reached behind him shutting off the water. He then carefully stepped out of the tub, all the while Abbie ground her pussy against his dick causing a deep moan to escape him.

He quickly walked them to the sink and plopped Abbie on top while devouring her mouth with his. When he felt Abbie's hand push at this chest he was surprised.

"Move," she growled, this time succeeding he took a step away from her. The moment he was about to reach for her though she shocked the shit out of him by dropping to her knees.

He had to blink a few times to make sure he saw it right. It was still dark after all.

"My turn," Abbie cooed from below him. The moment Hunter focused on her eyes though, he almost lost himself.

Before he could say anything, Abbie brought her lips to the tip of his member giving it a light kiss. Oh fuck, she was going to be the death of him. His whole body tensed.

Abbie kept her eyes locked on his as she brought him into her mouth. The amount of times Hunter had pictured this very same thing was nothing compared to the reality.

She pulled back with a pop. "Thick. I like it."

"Fuck, Abbie don't talk like that," he somehow managed to get out through clenched teeth.

"Why?"

"I'll come all over your face."

Abbie winked at him before giving the tip another kiss. "Who said I didn't want that?"

If he had any control before, it was gone now.

Then she started working him up and down.

He was seconds from losing it when Abbie did the unthinkable. She pulled her head back one last time before taking him fully into her mouth causing him to bottom out at the back of her throat.

"Fuck!" Hunter pushed his hips forward as his hands fisted her hair.

Dear god, this woman unmanned him.

Each time he felt himself touch the back of her throat he lost it more and more. At this point he was seconds from exploding deep down her throat, and although he would love to do just that, he had other plans.

As much as it pained him, he let go of her head before pulling himself out of her mouth.

"Hey, we were just getting to the good part!"

Hunter clenched his teeth. "Trust me, I know. But, I'm not coming in your mouth, Abbie. Not this time."

When she thrust out her bottom lip in protest Hunter growled again. "Put it back in or I'll bite it." Before she could say anything, Hunter grabbed under her arms pulling her onto her feet before placing her on top of the sink.

He spread her legs before dropping to his knees.

"*Noooo*," Abbie cried as she inched closer to the edge of the counter. "You. Inside me. Now!"

"Let me taste you first." *And get better control of my dick.* Hunter took one long lick down her slit before coming back up stopping at her clit.

"Oh god!"

He pulled it into his mouth as his right hand found her entrance. *Fuck, how was it possible she tasted this good?* As he worked her, he felt her legs shake.

"That's it, baby, come for me," he hummed around her clit causing her to scream out as her walls tightened around his fingers. "That's right, Abbie. *I'm* the one that makes you come like this. Never forget it." With that, he was on his feet positioning himself at her core.

Before Abbie could utter anything, he pushed himself inside her. Hunter bit his cheek to fight himself for control as Abbie's pussy clenched around him.

She reached for his hips urging him to go harder.

Oh, he'd go harder. Fuck, he loved this woman. He loved her fire, her passion. Everything about her.

He loved her.

Hunter grabbed her left leg and placed it on his shoulder as he slammed into her. Shit, he was close.

Using his other hand, he moved between them seeking out her nub. Once he found it, he started to rub with such force within seconds Abbie was squirming and shaking as she begged. "Please, Hunter, oh god I'm gonna come. Oh god!"

Her walls tightened. No matter how hard he tried he couldn't hold back. He looked deep into her eyes as he grunted out his release.

He didn't give a fuck if she got pregnant.

Actually, he wanted her to. And as her pussy milked every last drop from him, he wanted her to know that, too.

There was no way in hell he was ever letting her go again.

# CHAPTER TWENTY

Abbie sat on the edge of the sink in a complete daze as she fought to regain her breathing. Her heart rate was also dangerously high on the "about to have a heart attack" scale.

As she worked on calming herself, Abbie chanced a glance at Hunter.

She gulped.

Hunter's intense gaze unnerved her. There was something about those hunter green eyes that seemed like they were looking straight into her soul.

She didn't like it.

Sure, he'd spent a great deal of time giving her odd looks, but this was different.

"Umm," was all Abbie got out before Hunter's hands were at her waist pulling her off the sink. In fear of falling to her doom, she quickly wrapped her legs around him while she threw her arms around his neck. "What gives?"

"Shh," Hunter silenced her with a smack to her ass making Abbie clench her teeth.

His obsession with smacking her butt was getting tiresome. She wasn't an errant child and if he did it again, she was gonna smack his.

Although... that could be fun.

*No,* she scolded herself.

Hunter grabbed for the towel on the rack, casually wrapping it around her back while still in his arms. Abbie's brows went to the ceiling. However, the second Hunter took a step toward the bathroom door, her eyes bulged.

He was *still* inside her.

Every step he took, the sensation ricocheted through her body. Abbie bit her bottom lip to stop herself from moaning.

What the hell was wrong with her?

Hunter, seemingly unaffected, walked them over to the bed before gently placing her down. As he stepped back, he slowly withdrew. Her betraying body sent a chill down her spine at the loss of him.

Then, she felt wetness, a thick wetness spill between her legs.

*You've got to be kidding me!* She wanted to punch herself, and then Hunter as the reality set in.

They'd fought, fucked, and then that asshole came in her, not once but *twice!*

Holy fucking crap on all the crackers. Abbie was going to kill him. Did he give zero shits of the consequences of his actions? There was no way in hell either of them was ready to have a child.

Her anger came back with force. Fuck him, and fuck this, and while she was at it, fuck herself for being so caught up in Hunter she didn't use her goddamn common sense.

However, when Abbie tried to roll away from him, she immediately found herself being pounced on. Her arms were pinned over her head in a move that Abbie now understood as Hunter's go-to. "You're not going anywhere this time, Abbie."

This was ridiculous. "Get off me, Hunter."

"No, I like you better when you're under me." He smirked.

"You can't go around pinning me all the time to get your way. That's not how adults act."

Hunter cocked his brow. "You lunge at me anytime you get the chance."

"That's different." She pushed trying to loosen his hold, but failed. "Get off me. I mean it."

"No." Abbie wanted to punch the smug look off his face. "I'm not letting you go while you have that look in your eyes."

Her brows pulled together as her eyes hardened. "What look? The look of murder? 'Cause that's the only look I should have."

Seemingly unfazed by her threat Hunter's smile spread from ear-to-ear. "Nah, that's your resting face. I'm talking about the look you've got right now."

"Oh, pray tell, old wise one. What look do *I* have? Not like I would know or anything since it's *my* face and all."

Hunter leaned forward and kissed her nose causing Abbie to growl. "I'll bite you."

"My little zombie. I didn't know you were into biting but we can try that."

*If I murder him, Universe, can you bring him back to life so I can murder him all over again?*

"Ahh, there's the look I've grown to love." Hunter beamed. "What are you thinking of stabbing me with? Knife, pen, a rusty spoon, maybe a book?"

A menacing noise echoed from Abbie's throat.

"Growl all you want, Abs. I'm not letting you go. I've

decided we've had enough games. We're having this conversation." For good measure, the jerk kissed her once more.

"Stop doing that, Hunter. Don't you get how bad this is? All of it. We've had sex and you *came* in me!"

"I know." He smirked. "Twice."

The glee in his eyes unhinged Abbie. "I'm not on anything, ass-hat."

"So you've said."

What seventh level of hell was this? She fought against his hold. "Have you lost your fucking mind?"

"When it comes to you? Yes. But I kinda like it lost."

How could he be so calm about this? This wasn't some stupid childhood dare. No, this was their life at stake. This isn't a game. "I don't want to be a mother right now, Hunter. And most of all, I don't want *you* to be the father. This is *serious*. So start acting like it."

He placed his hand on his chest like he'd been shot. "That hurts."

"Really, why do you have to be like that?"

"If I believed even for a second you meant what you just said, I would. But you don't." He shrugged.

Abbie's jaw hit the ground. "You pompous egotistical, asshole." She couldn't handle this anymore. Her eyes snapped shut as her hand went to her stomach. She felt as though she was drowning. "I could be pregnant." Tears pricked her eyes in frustration.

"And if you are, we'll take care of it. I never really thought about being a dad before, but I'm not opposed to it now. I am getting older after all."

As Abbie fought back her tears, out of nowhere an image of Hunter playing with a small child that looked exactly like a mix of them entered her mind. Her heart tightened. *No, no, no!* She didn't want children.

Her heart broke for the thought of her child growing up as she did. What if Hunter left just like her dad did? Everything inside of her shattered at the thought of her baby feeling what she'd felt her whole life.

Hunter had already left once, he'd do it again.

Hell, he'd already done that when they were kids.

Children weren't in the cards for her. Rupert was enough.

"Let's take it one day at a time," Hunter said distracting Abbie from her thoughts. "Being a parent is scary, I get that," he spoke softly. "Although, I do have to mention the *rat* you mother is also pretty scary. Not to mention your track record with plants has me a little weary, but—"

"Do not bring Rupert or my garden into this." Her eyes shot open. "This is about us creating a life. A life neither one of us are ready for." She glared. "And, for your information, I'm the best damn cat mom there ever was. I'd be a great mom." *Asshole.*

"And your plants?" Hunter smirked.

"Shut up."

They stared at each other for a few seconds before Hunter let out a sigh. "Let's at least wait until the storm is over. If you really want to take the pill, we'll go get it together."

Hearing his words was like a weight lifted off her shoulders. Finally, a glimmer of hope was there.

"And in the meantime, we'll use condoms. They have some in the lobby's corner store." Hunter's smile went from ear-to-ear as her mouth fell open in a loss for words.

How had her life come to this exact moment? Her whole world was crashing around her, and she had no idea how to make it stop.

After Hunter left her standing in her driveway all those years ago, she was never supposed to see him again.

She never *wanted* to see him again.

And as far as Abbie was concerned, Hunter died on some street corner after daring the wrong guy something insane.

That's how she got through the nights when he'd pop back into her head. That's how she dealt with the gaping hole that was left in her heart the moment he walked away from her.

Abbie swallowed hard as all the things she'd hidden away came crashing to the surface.

Hunter was the bane of her existence growing up. He *made* her like him in some sick and twisted fashion, and then he ripped out her heart and stomped on it, making her the laughing stock of the whole school. But that wasn't the worst part.

No.

The jab about her dad was the last straw.

It was the one thing that broke her.

From that moment on, Abbie changed.

She guessed she had Hunter to thank for that. If it weren't for him, she'd still be that happy-go-lucky naïve girl that thought everyone was good, unicorns farted rainbows, and the only bad guy there was, and ever would be was her father.

That day in her driveway, Hunter taught her the opposite. There were more of her "fathers" in the world than there were of her.

As her heart clenched, she mustered up her voice. "Why are you here, Hunter?"

"There's a hurricane outside." He cocked his brow.

Was he always this obtuse? "No, dumbass. Uhh, why are you so difficult?"

Hunter's eyes widened. "*I'm* the difficult one?"

"Yes, you are. You know damn well what I'm asking you. Why did you come back into my life?"

As she waited for her answer, the room fell silent.

After what felt like an eternity, Hunter finally spoke. "For you, Abbie. I came back for you."

At his words Abbie's heart did that stupid flip again right before it shattered into unrepairable pieces.

It wasn't true.

"Abbie, look at me."

She couldn't.

She wouldn't. Not while everything she'd ever built inside her for protection was falling apart.

"Abbie," Hunter warned in a serious tone causing her to actually look at him. When she saw the clear pain in his eyes, everything stopped.

"I came back for you, Abbie."

No! She wouldn't believe it. She snapped her head to the side as anger ran through her at his anguish.

Hunter had no right to have pain. *He's* the one that did this. He's the one that left and took her fucking heart with him. He's the one that killed who she once was. "I hate you."

"I hated you too."

Her breath caught as she darted her eyes to him in shock.

"I hated everything about you, Abbie." The pain in his words were enough to choke her. "But then I realized it wasn't hate. It was the furthest thing from hate."

"Stop," she begged.

"It was love, Abs. It's always been love. I loved you,

Abbie. I still do. I *am* in love with you Abigail Collins and I have been since we were ten."

"Stop it. Stop it right now!" Tears poured from her eyes. "Please, please, stop."

"You asked me why I came back, I'm telling you the answer. I love you."

Abbie shook her head back and forth trying to dismiss Hunter's words as pain coursed through her. "You can't say you loved me then and you love me now. No. I don't believe you, Hunter. Love doesn't make someone spread rumors all around school. Love doesn't torment. Love doesn't look you in the eye and say you aren't good enough."

All the pain she felt on that day as his words cut through her came back like a brick to the face. "If I wasn't good enough for my dad, I'll never be good enough for anyone."

# CHAPTER TWENTY-ONE

HEARING her words and seeing the tears cascading down Abbie's cheeks were a knife straight to Hunter's gut. God, he hated himself for what he'd said to her.

Not a day went by that he hadn't thought of that scene in her driveway.

Hunter released her like her wrists were on fire and he'd just been burnt. He sat back on his ankles as Abbie scurried away from him pushing away her tears.

He forced himself to keep his eyes focused on her. This is what he had done. This is what he had done to her with his outlandish words.

The words he never meant.

The words he regretted every single day of his life.

Hunter carefully crawled closer to Abbie as he reached out his hand to wipe away a tear. "Abbie, baby…"

She pushed his hand away. "No. You don't get to do that. You never get to do that."

Hunter pulled back with a sigh. "Let me explain, please?" How could he, though? No words would ever justify what he'd done. He'd never hated himself more than he did at this moment.

"Explain what, Hunter? That when we were kids, your only goal was to tease and dare me until I kissed you? Then you could be an asshole to me?" Her eyes hardened. "Is that what you're going to tell me? The sick, unhealthy codependent friendship we formed was all a part of this massive plan to humiliate me? Oh, wait, that was just the icing on the cake, right? It's been your plan all along to find me once we were adults just to rub salt in the wound that never healed?"

Hunter held up his hands. "It's not like that."

"Whatever you have to say will never change the fact that I hate you. I hate everything about you. You are nothing but a—"

Hunter silenced her with a kiss.

What else could he do? And honestly, she needed to stop talking for a few seconds while he gathered his thoughts. Besides, if she really had that much hatred toward him, which he *knew* she didn't. He had to at least explain the situation, even if it was one-hundred percent shitty on his part. "Your time for talking is over."

"Excuse me?" her brows shot to the ceiling.

Hunter held her hands at her side as he stole another quick kiss. He couldn't be blamed for seizing the opportunity. For all he knew, she was liable to finally follow through on all her threats. "It's time we had this talk. We've got some air to clear."

"Clear the air? I ought to—" He silenced her with his lips once more. Who was he kidding? This was Abbie. Strong arming was the *only* way to deal with her. "This will be the last time I do it with my lips." Hunter raised his hand.

When Abbie's mouth fell open, he fought back his smile. However, when she glared at him, he did smile. Putting aside her adorable anger issues, this was serious. He took a calming breath before he began. "What I said to you in your driveway was horrible. There is absolutely no excuse for it. I've replayed that conversation over a million times in my head. When I'm lying in bed at night wondering what you are doing. It pops up. Walking down the street. It's there. When I'm at the bar and an attractive woman approaches me. It's your devastated face I see. When I'm seconds from coming with my hand wrapped around my dick, your face pops into my head and I lose it. I lose it all because the girl I wanted to spend all my days and nights with thinks I didn't want her. There is not a day that goes by that I don't think about it. It was the most asshole thing I had ever done.... And doing it to *you* was inexcusable."

Abbie stared at him while her mouth opened and closed. "I don't... why?"

Hunter cleared his throat as he recalled the memory. "A few days before that kiss, I came home to find my stepmom sleeping with her gym trainer."

"*What?*"

"Yeah," he laughed. "Right there in the living room. At first, I wasn't sure if what I was seeing was right, but the sounds they were making were undeniable." Hunter looked Abbie in the eyes. "She saw me you know, over the guy's shoulder. Fuck, Abbie, she winked at me. I turned and ran out of the house so fast I probably broke a world record. I was at a complete loss."

"Hunter..."

"I told my dad that night," he continued. "He was pissed. And rightly so. It was a mess. That night everything changed. And before I knew it, we were moving. Dad wanted absolutely nothing to do with her, especially after he confronted my stepmom and she shrugged it off. So we packed our bags and had one week to wrap everything up before my dad's transfer went through."

"Is that why you said you weren't going to prom?" she asked, grabbing the nearby pillow to cover herself. And, this was one of the many reasons he loved her. No matter what she was feeling toward him right now, she hung on to every word he said, just like a best friend would. Just as she did back then.

Hunter nodded. "That day I was leaving the coach's office after telling him I was dropping the team. I was pissed, I was angry at everything and everyone. I didn't understand why she would do that to my dad, or how I was the one who had to find out. Or, better yet, why were we the ones being punished. Because of *her,* my whole life was changing in the blink of an eye. Then I saw you sitting there."

Hunter rubbed the back of his neck while a chuckle escaped him. "It's funny. I loved you back then and I didn't even know it." He shook his head. "You always made everything better, Abbie. You were always on my mind. Every spare second I had was consumed with thinking up dares for you. Hell, I didn't care if you did them or not, I just wanted to be near you, however sick and twisted that was. I knew sitting with you would help ease some of what I was feeling."

Abbie looked like he'd slapped her, but it was true. He didn't fully understand it at the time.

Now he did.

Abbie had always been his everything.

Hunter looked back into her eyes. "When I sat down

next to you, the thought of leaving and never kissing you, even once, consumed me with dread. I didn't know why, but I had to."

Abbie's brows drew together. "If what you're saying is true, why did you purposely hurt me?"

He turned away, ashamed. "When we got caught I ... I have no clue. I was a stupid kid. I don't know why I said what I did. All my emotions were fucked and seeing you sitting there all perfect like you always were and here I was struggling to get by in school, my home life was now like stepping on a land mine. I just—"

"My life was never perfect, Hunter. I was always a mess. I pushed and pushed to do well so my mom wouldn't have to worry. She was already working two jobs just trying to support us all 'cause my dad left. Plus, I was always in this stupid dare-off with my neighbor." And like it was the piece of hope Hunter begged for, Abbie sent him a small side smile.

"And here you are, once again, proving how perfect you are trying to lighten the mood."

She shook her head. "I'm just trying to understand. You could have told me what happened, Hunter. I don't know what help I could have been, but I would have at least been there for you. You didn't have to say the things you did."

"I wanted you to hate me. Like I hated me. When we stood outside of your house, I knew if I succeeded and said the worst possible thing I could think of at the time, I would survive. If you hated me, I foolishly thought it would be easier to walk away from you." His face softened. "But it wasn't. I could never walk away from you, Abbie. Not then and not now."

As the wind and rain pelted the window, neither of

them spoke. How could he? Anytime he thought of the past, he hated himself more and more.

"You wanted me to hate you?" Abbie's voice broke through his thoughts. "I think I understand that, I'm trying to. But you didn't have to spread the rumors around school. I couldn't walk onto school grounds without being bullied."

Hunter sat back as his brow's pulled together. "What rumors?"

"Abbie flabby likes it on her backie," she mocked. "Or, how about the ones where people needed to stay away from me since I had STDs 'cause I was so easy." She rolled her eyes. "People actually cowered away from me in the halls."

Hunter's eyes widened. "Abbie, I never once said any of that."

"Pfft," she snorted. "Yeah, right."

"Abbie, we left five minutes after I walked out of your driveway. I never stepped back onto campus again."

The room fell into silence as the storm raged on outside. Hunter remained quiet for a few moments as he thought back.

After moving, he never stayed in contact with anyone, he'd never heard about any rumors or... *wait a second.* As Hunter recalled the day after the kiss, he remembered going into the locker room to clean out his stuff. There was a group of boys with Troy all laughing. When he walked by them, some of the guys had even given him high-fives and said stuff like, *legend,* and *I can't believe it.* Hunter hadn't thought much of it.

Actually, truth be told, he thought it was some sort of goodbye thing since the coach had announced his leaving earlier that day.

But now, that he really thought about it, he remembered Troy giving him a weird smile.

That's when everything started to fall into place. Troy was not only the teammate that caught him and Abbie, but he was also the school's primary source of gossip. As everything pieced together his fists clenched. "If I see him again, I'll rip out his throat."

"What?"

"Abbie." Hunter jumped to his feet causing his dangly bit to flop around, but he didn't give a shit. He was pissed. "I take full responsibility for the shit I said to you in your driveway and after the kiss. If you need to keep on hating me for that fine, I will do everything in my power for you to learn to forgive me. But I never once spread rumors about you at school but I know who did." Fuck Hunter wanted to punch something.

No wonder Abbie hated him. It wasn't just what he'd said, no, it was way worse than that. She had to endure spiteful teenagers. Damnit, he was pissed. Pissed at himself. Pissed at the situation, and pissed at Troy. If he ever saw him again, he'd break him in two.

"Who?"

"Fucking Troy," Hunter growled as he paced.

"Oh," Abbie said.

"I will hunt him down and bury him."

When Hunter heard Abbie snort with a laugh he stopped pacing and turned toward her. She had this huge smile on her face.

*What the fuck?*

"No need," Abbie announced squaring her shoulders with pride. "Troy and I actually ended up at the same college."

"You did?" Hunter cocked his head as he walked back to the bed before sitting.

"Yeah, although, since I graduated early I was ahead of him."

"Okay..."

"One day I was walking around campus and I just so happened to hear the words Abbie and flabby together."

Hunter saw red.

"Down, killer." Abbie held up her hands. "I took care of him."

"What did you do?" The only answer he would accept at this point was murder.

"When I turned I saw who it was. I didn't know he went there, but the second he saw me Troy tried making me the butt of the joke around his friends. I had my calculus book in my hands. I smacked him so hard across the head with it, I knocked him out for a few seconds."

Hunter's eyes widened as his jaw hit the floor. "I'm impressed."

"Don't be," she laughed. "If it was my economics book, then you can be impressed, that thing was big. I swear it's the reason I had back problems in college."

Hunter let out a small laugh. "Okay, so what happened?" *Holy shit.*

Abbie shrugged. "When he came to, I had his shirt in my fist. I warned him if he ever said another word about me to anyone I would hunt him down and gut him *and* do it with a smile on my face."

A chill ran down Hunter's spine. "I see your violence has always been an issue. You really ought to talk to someone about that."

Abbie winked. "What can I say, after the incident with you, I decided *no one* would ever make me feel less. And if that meant a couple of five knuckle sandwiches, I was fine with that."

That got Hunter's attention in more ways than one. He hated he was the cause of her distress, but he was damn proud she stood up for herself. Seeing Abbie's half-smile, he cocked his head to the side. "Abbie, did you ever hit anyone else?"

"Me? No. Of course not," she innocently said.

"Abbie..."

"No." She shrugged. "After I knocked him out with the textbook, rumors got around and people left me alone. That was the way I liked it back then. I didn't need anyone's approval, friendship or anything anymore. I was only focused on one thing, being the best I could be and you didn't need people crowding around you to do that."

His heart broke for her. The Abbie of their younger years would have made it her mission to find a friend in anyone. Hunter ruined that for her and he vowed at this very moment to stop at nothing to fix all that he'd done.

"Nothing happened to me thankfully," she said interrupting his thoughts. "I kept my head down and worked my ass off to get to where I am today."

Hunter knew that. Well, he didn't know about the rumors or that she knocked the fuck out of Troy... he should reward her for that.

Maybe with his tongue, he thought. He shook his head, getting back on track. "I know," he announced storing the idea in his head for later.

"You do?"

"Yeah. After I stopped being angry, I looked for you. I kept tabs on you the whole time. I was just waiting for the right moment to come back."

Abbie's eyebrows shot to the ceiling. "Instead of sending an email like, "Hey how have you been?" you decide to show up on one of the most important career days of my life and be a dick? You planned that?"

"Oh, my dick did something that day. But no, it just so happened to work out the way it did. Why did you walk in with your tits hanging out, anyway?"

"I didn't do it on purpose, okay?" Abbie shook her head. "I was mortified at the sequence of events that morning but at that point it was either pull up my big girl panties and kill it or run away and cry. A Collins never backs down and never surrenders. So, tits out it was."

They both shared a laugh as the room once again fell into silence. Hunter didn't know where to go from here. And as Abbie was locked in her own thoughts he doubted she did either.

But something changed between them, Hunter could feel it.

The tension was still there, but not like before. And as soon as everything settled, he was going to stop at nothing to prove to Abbie he was here for the long haul. No matter how long it took.

Taking a chance, Hunter glanced at Abbie. That's when he realized she was staring at him.

The tension built as her mouth hung slightly opened. "Hunter," Abbie's voice pierced through the room. "I dare you."

"You dare me to what?" His heart sped as his breathing increased.

"Kiss me."

# CHAPTER TWENTY-TWO

ABBIE'S HEART raced as she sat in her seat on the plane. She should have been expecting it, but the thoughts of imminent death still crept through her.

One safe flight did not mean she could cheat death twice. She wasn't stupid.

Abbie looked out the window. Yeah, the window. Hunter had insisted she sit on the inside this time. Sure, there was a part of her that liked the security of the wall and Hunter on either side, but that meant if the plane was falling to a fiery death she was trapped.

Not that she would survive it either way, but she at least liked the option of not being wedged between a hunk of metal and a hunk of man meat.

She smacked her hand to her forehead. Did she really just compare Hunter to a hunk of man meat?

Freaking great.

What had the last thirty-five hours done to her brain? Sex made her stupid.

As the plane moved from the gate, Abbie's hands shook.

That's when she felt Hunter pull her left hand to his lips lightly kissing the back. Her eyes followed their movement.

It was still kind of surreal to her.

Actually, all of this was surreal. How had she gone from years of pent up anger at Hunter to now banging his brains out? Although, that anger did make for some killer passion, but the more she thought about it the more her head hurt.

Her mind wasn't fully wrapped around everything yet, but she was getting there.

Hell, her heart had already decided to give Hunter a chance and even though her mind sometimes fought against it, she was willing to try.

After all, the sex was phenomenal. Angry sex was the best sex. Abbie couldn't count the number of times he made her come while the storm raged on. That being said, angry sex she understood. It was the painfully slow, tender sex that now played a part she couldn't fathom.

Hunter explored every inch of her body, and he did it in such a way, she would be a fool to deny his feelings for her. She didn't really know how to make sense of it. The parts of her body she hated he'd spent extra time on, the parts she loved, he spent extra time on.

It was like he wanted all of her. Every last bit, and that was a new concept.

Who the heck went around thinking people were whole just the way they were? Not with TV and movies shoving crap down your throat.

With a sigh, Abbie looked back at Hunter. Gahhh, what was wrong with her? See, sex did make her stupid. Any other time she'd be off in her own little delusional world but no, Hunter brought her to this weird reality and she wasn't sure she liked it.

Abbie shook her head to remove the thoughts. No use in

thinking about it now. She had to make a list of the people she planned on haunting once the plane crashed.

*Bill.*

*Troy.*

*The mailman who always gave her the wrong mail.*

*Hunter.*

Abbie wanted to drive back, but no, big headed Hunter insisted they fly. Once the storm was over, and they got the all-clear to check out the area. There were trees down and debris everywhere, it would have been a mess to try and navigate through. So, Hunter said.

Abbie was all ready to pull some sick ass maneuvers around fallen trees, maybe show off some of those newly acquired ninja skills. Before she could convince him though, the jerk bought two tickets on the next plane out, once the airport opened.

But in all the mess she at least got to see Doug the driver again. In some weird twisted sense of humor from the Universe, he was the car that pulled up to take them to the airport.

A wicked smile appeared on her face.

Abbie would never get the look of amusement Doug had or mortification Hunter sported after she proudly announced Hunter did *not* have gross hairy balls.

Highlight of the trip so far.

And Hunter's promise to get her back once they got home sent a wave of excitement through her. She'd never admit it, but she liked when Hunter pinned her down.

She'd take that to the grave, though.

No need to inflate his ego any more than it already was.

Plus, ninety-five percent of the time she still wanted to throat punch him. The other five percent she wanted to fuck him, is this what a relationship was? Oh, god, she swallowed. Did this make Hunter her *boyfriend?*

Her head spun.

*Abbie, this is one of those times you don't put a label on things. Instead, you're just gonna tuck all this away and deal with it later. Right now, you have more important things to worry about anyway. Like recalling all movies and tv shows were people ended up stranded on desert islands and take notes on how they survived.*

The plane ran over a bump causing her stomach to bottom out. "Oh god, it's happening again."

"Why don't you read the book you just bought?" Hunter interrupted her panic as he nudged her with his shoulder.

With her free hand, Abbie held up the book. "This is for when we're *in* the air, not taking off. Taking off is for completely irrational and overdramatic thoughts of impending doom. Didn't you get that the first time?"

"I'm glad we've reached the level in our relationship where you show 'your' crazy."

Abbie smacked the book with his chest. "Hey!"

"Kidding. Kidding." Hunter shook his head with a chuckle. "You've always shown 'your' crazy. It's one of the things I love about you. No pretending, instead I'm getting the real deal upfront." When he smirked at her, Abbie's eyes narrowed which only caused Hunter to lean over and plant a kiss on her lips.

"Besides from the cover it looks like someone's about to *take off,* if you know what I mean." He waggled his brows as he snatched the book from her hand. "Hank and his Fireman's Hose by Quinn Sparks." Hunter chuckled as he flipped it over. "Look at the praise: Hank knew exactly what to do with his *hose* to send shivers down my back! Quinn

Sparks has done it again with this five-star read. Oh, and there is a cat the size of a human child that stole the show. I've never laughed so hard in my life." Hunter looked at Abbie. "Is this the blurb that made it say *buy me?*"

There was pure amusement in his eyes. It made her want to uppercut him. However, with her promise to be less violent when it came to Hunter, instead she snatched the book out of his hands. "No, it's this pantie dropping dude on the cover. You see the way he's holding that firehose? Makes me want to set fire to my kitchen."

Hunter's eyes darkened as a low moan escaped him. "Say the word and I'll find a fireman's costume. I'm not opposed to role play."

Abbie shook her head. "Pig."

"But I'm your pig," Hunter said with a laugh as he puffed out his chest.

"Don't remind me. I'm still trying to figure out how we are now in some sick and twisted relationship."

"We've always been in a sick and twisted relationship. Now there's just sex involved."

She rolled her eyes so hard she thought she'd give herself a migraine. That's when she realized exactly what Hunter was doing.

He was very good at distracting her.

"We're clear for take-off."

All the color drained from Abbie's face as chills ran through her body. She quickly placed her book in the pocket in front of her before pulling on her seatbelt for the five thousandth time.

*Being next to the window did that mean there was some possibility for negative pressure? Am I going to be sucked out? What if there is a crack in the window and no one noticed it?* That was a thing, right? People getting sucked out of windows. She swore she's seen it in at least three movies.

However, the second she felt tears prick the back of her eyes, something was placed over her lap. When she looked down she saw a black blanket over her legs and a toothy grin coming from Hunter. He then lifted the armrest between them before scooting his lower half under the blanket with her.

"What are you doing?" she snapped. "This isn't a time for a nap. We're about to die."

Hunter barked out a laugh before giving her his famous smirk. The one that still made her want to punch him. "No. What *I'm* about to do is distract you."

"By tucking me in? Newsflash, Hunter, my ass is not going to sleep." She stared at him in disbelief. Maybe venturing into a relationship with him was not the smartest idea. The sex be damned.

Hunter's hand snaked under the blanket before landing on Abbie's thigh. He gave it a firm squeeze as he looked her in the eyes. "I have no intention of you going to sleep, babe."

*What?*

The moment Hunter's hand trailed up her leg and to the waistband of her leggings her eyes bulged. He was not about to do what she thought he was? No, way, no way in—

"Relax." Abbie's eyes widened as she felt Hunter's hand move to the top of her pants.

"Hunter..." she warned.

"Shh, no talking from you." Before she could say anything, Hunter's hand slipped between the material.

*Oh god, he wasn't serious, was he? No, there was no way—*

Hunter's hand stroked up and down her panties. *Yep, he was doing this.*

"Relax, baby." He leaned over kissing the side of her neck. "Let me distract you. I wanted to do this for you the first time. Let me do it now."

"People will see," she whispered right as Hunter pushed aside her panties touching her now swollen lips with his fingertips.

"No, they won't." He kissed her neck. "Everyone is in their seats and my body is blocking the view. Plus, there's a blanket." He flipped the blanket up with the top of his hand.

"Is this why you wanted me to sit by the window?" She clenched her teeth as his finger grazed her clit.

"That was my plan." Before Abbie could say another word, Hunter brought his lips to her neck and bit causing her to let out a tiny gasp.

"Open for me."

And the hussy inside of her did.

Abbie scooted her butt forward on her seat as she let her legs fall open. *Holy crap on crackers, this felt wrong.*

He slowly spread her lips seeking out better access to her pussy. "Shimmy your pants down," he whispered into her ear.

"Are you insane? Heck no."

"Yes."

"Yes, you're insane? Good, we're in agreement." She glanced behind him, but thankfully didn't see anyone looking their way.

"Lift up and pull them down a few inches, Abbie," he demanded. "I won't tell you again."

"What do you mean you *won't tell me again*, are you threatening me?" She cocked her brow. "What do you think you're gonna do, 'cause I will rip off your dick and make you eat—"

A gasp escaped her lips the second Hunter pinched her clit. Her hand shot to her mouth as she tried her best to keep herself quiet.

*Holy shit.*

Her body hummed as he worked her. *Oh, god, oh, god, oh, freaking god!* Abbie held her eyes tightly closed as she fought her body. There were people less than a few feet from them. This was the stupidest thing she'd ever done.

A wave of desire ran through her as he continued to stroke her core.

Could she do this?

That's when Hunter's fingers pushed between her folds.

Yeah, she could do this!

Abbie pushed on her heels giving her butt extra room. Hunter then grabbed the waistband of her leggings before pulling them down her thighs a few inches. He slipped his hand inside her panties again seeking out her center.

"Hunter," she panted as two of his fingers slid inside her, while his thumb found her clit.

She bit the bottom of her cheek so hard Abbie swore she tasted blood.

"Let go, baby." He whispered as he worked her under the blanket.

She couldn't, not while they were surrounded by so many people. However, the second she opened her eyes and looked at Hunter, she was a goner. She couldn't hold back even if she tried. The moment he found her spot and pressed down, her legs shook.

Instantly, his mouth was on her lips silencing her cry as her release rocked through her.

He continued to work her as she rode out her orgasm. When the last shakes subsided, she sat back in a daze.

*Holy crapolie.*

Hunter carefully removed his fingers from her core before bringing them to his mouth. She watched in awe as he took each finger and licked them one by one.

*Whoa.*

Abbie's eyes moved to Hunter's waist. She could clearly see the evidence of his arousal under the blanket.

Should she? Is this what you do in relationships, you get each other off a billion miles from the ground?

"Later," Hunter answered like he'd read her mind.

Abbie blinked at him.

"As soon as we land and get back to your house, I plan on sinking so deep inside of you that you'll forget what it's like to *not* have my dick in you."

*What?* And more importantly why did that send a new wave of wetness to her core. Oh god, Hunter had completely corrupted her.

And she liked it.

"Pull your pants up." A devilish smile appeared on his face as he winked her way.

*Ahhh,* that's right her pants were halfway down her thighs. That snapped her thoughts out of what Hunter could do to her and on every surface of her house.

Blah! Abbie was sitting on an airplane seat. Then reality hit her. *Eww, eww, ewwwww!* As quick as she could she pulled up her pants before tossing the blanket at Hunter's face. "Do you know how unsanitary that was?" She faked a gag. "I'm gonna vom."

Hunter shrugged as he laughed. "You're very dramatic. We kept your panties on so no bare ass touched the seat. Plus..." A wicked smile appeared on his face. "We're in the air, now aren't we?"

Abbie shot her head to the window as she saw the

clouds rolling by. Holy shit, they were in the air. She hadn't even noticed they left the ground.

Abbie turned back to Hunter, who had a shit-eating grin on his face. Damn, he was good. And if this was how take-offs and landings were going to be from now on, then she for sure could get used to flying.

# CHAPTER TWENTY-THREE

HUNTER WATCHED Abbie's ass as they walked up the steps to her house. He didn't even try to hide his groan. Her ass was the homing beacon he would gladly follow anywhere and he didn't give a shit who knew it.

Hunter's mouth watered at Abbie's curves, her laughter, her feistiness. Every time she threatened to punch him, it was like a fire right to his groin.

But there was one problem.

He knew Abbie, and even though she *seemed* okay with this development between them, she wasn't. Well, that wasn't true, she was clearly on board for the sex, but believing he was serious about this?

No.

He'd known her long enough to realize she'd compartmentalized them in her head and that wasn't going to do.

Hunter was in this for the long haul and the sooner Abbie realized that, the better.

Abbie was it for him.

Before he agreed to the trial period with WCM; along with the fact his old boss had practically pushed him out the door and told him to go get his girl, he knew this was his end game. Where Abbie was, he was. If only he could make her understand that.

"Mommy's home!" Abbie screamed as she threw open the front door.

*Oh shit,* how could he have forgotten about the alien creature? Then like out of some bad sci-fi movie Rupert ran full speed around the corner and right into Abbie's arms. Where she then proceeded to smother it with kisses and cooed at him.

Fuck, if Abbie would greet him like that, he'd strip down naked and only wear a turtleneck. Actually, now that he thought about it, that was exactly something he would do.

"Did you miss your mommy?" Abbie made loud smacking kisses on its wrinkly head. "My baby, I missed you so much."

Okay, now that was creepy.

"Were you a good boy for Grandma? Were you? I bet you were the best little man there ever was."

"He clawed my leg, bit my arm, and then demanded to wear the pink turtleneck instead of the purple one I put on him."

Hunter's head shot to where he heard the voice. That's when he saw Abbie's mother appear from the kitchen.

"He was an asshole. But for him, he was good."

"Hey, Mom," Abbie said walking to her before kissing her cheek. "Glad to know Rupert likes to put everyone in their place and not just me."

Kathleen laughed. "Technically, he should be in timeout right now. He knocked down a plant that was on the windowsill."

"Oh no, is Clark dead?" Abbie pushed past her mother

and into the kitchen.

"Who's Clark?"

"That's the name I gave the plant Hunter saved."

"Why did you name it when it's only going to die?"

Abbie ran back into the living room with the plant in her arms. "Mom!"

"What?"

"Don't say that."

Kathleen shrugged. "I don't know why you get all angry when I'm only speaking the truth."

Abbie's mouth fell open. "My own mother. I never thought I'd see the day."

"Sure you did, honey." She pat Abbie on the shoulder. "As your mother, I have to point out your difficulties."

"No, you don't!"

"It's in the mother handbook. You'll understand one day." Kathleen turned her attention to Hunter who had been leaning against the front door avidly watching them. "Speaking of which. Well, I'll be damned. Hunter James in the flesh, right in the front door of my daughter's home."

When she looked him up and down an uneasiness ran through him. "It's good to see you again, Mrs. Collins."

"It's Daniels now, but it's nice to see you again too, Hunter." She crossed her arms over her chest. "When Abbie said it was *you* she was working with, I have to admit I was a little surprised."

"Imagine how surprised *I* was," Abbie mumbled as she placed the plant on the coffee table.

All right, this was a tad awkward. That piercing stare from Kathleen had Hunter clearing his throat.

"So, Hunter James ..."

"Mom," Abbie warned.

"What? I only said his name."

"Yeah, but you said it in that weird way. The not good way."

"Sure I did, honey." She turned her stare back on him. "Now, Hunter, can you tell me why you decided it was a good idea to humiliate my daughter?"

"*Mom!*"

Hunter choked on his spit.

"It's a legitimate question. I want to know why he thought it was a good idea to make my baby girl cry?" She shook her head. "It's because of him you got all angry. Before Hunter you were as sweet as pie. Then you started threatening to punch anyone that pissed you off. Come to think of it." She tapped her finger on her chin. "You actually did punch someone once or twice."

Hunter looked to Abbie who had her arms crossed over her chest the exact same way her mother did. *Oh, shit.*

"Yeah, Hunter, I'd like to hear this too."

He narrowed his eyes at Abbie. As soon as he could she was gonna regret that.

"Well, you see, Mrs. Daniels I was an idiot child. If you ask Abbie she will probably say I'm still an idiot. The way I treated her when we were kids was inexcusable. I apologize for that." He turned to Abbie. "And I will never stop apologizing to you." He stared at her trying his best to convey his sincerity.

"Oh, really now?" Kathleen cocked her head slightly to the side. "What an interesting turn of events." She looked from him to Abbie a few times. Yeah, he didn't like this.

"Mom stop giving him the third degree. As much as it pains me to say this, Hunter and I are good now."

"Is it because of the sex?"

"*Mom!* What the hell?"

"Don't mom me. I wasn't born yesterday, missy. The

way that man just looked at you..." The corner of her mouth turned up in a devilish grin. "It was like you could read into his soul."

"Oh my god, you did *not* just say that!"

"What's the big deal? Sex is a very natural thing, sweetie. Until that day you came into the house crying I would have bet good money you and Hunter we're going to get together." Her smile spread from ear-to-ear.

"Stop talking."

"So, you're not having sex with him?" Kathleen turned toward Hunter. "I'm disappointed in you."

A wicked smile appeared on Hunter's face. "We're having sex."

"Holy fuck, both of you shut up!" Abbie threw her hands in the air. "How is this happening right now?"

"Do her random bursts of outrage concern you, as they do me?" Kathleen asked smiling at Hunter.

Holy shit she was awesome. "Sometimes," he answered.

"Maybe it's time for an intervention."

Hunter nodded. "It could be arranged."

"That's it, get out." Abbie pushed her mother toward the door. "You are no longer welcome in this house. Bye."

"Pity. Just when we were getting to the good part." Kathleen laughed as Abbie escorted her to the front door. When they passed Hunter though, she stopped. "If you ever do anything to my daughter again, I will hunt you down and gut you like a pig. We clear?" She poked him in the chest causing Hunter to step back.

What the hell? A shiver ran down his spine. With the look of determination in Kathleen's eyes, Hunter now knew where Abbie got it from. "Understood."

"Good." Kathleen opened the door before turning back to them. "Dinner is at six on Saturday. I expect you both to be there. Tootles." With that, she turned and slammed the door behind her.

"What the fuck just happened?" Hunter stared at the door.

"I honestly have no idea."

He barked out a deep laugh. "I like her. I don't remember her being this fun before."

"That's 'cause you were too busy being a jerk." She crossed her arms over her chest.

Hunter smirked as he stalked over to her. When he was toe-to-toe with Abbie he growled. "I have a promise to fulfill."

Her breath hitched. "And what's that?"

"My dick being so deep inside of you, you'll never forget I was there." Before she could say anything, his lips were on her.

Maybe it was the insanity of the situation or whatnot, but he had to have her. He peppered kisses down her neck. The moment her hand snaked between them to cup his member he grabbed it. "Don't. I'm about to explode. Making you come twice on the plane was enough to throw me over the edge. If you so much as look at my dick I'm gonna come."

"That could be fun."

"Not for you." His lips were back on hers as he devoured her with his kiss.

Rupert meowed from behind him causing him to jump. "Holy shit that thing scares me."

"Ignore him. Less talking more kissing." Abbie pulled his collar bringing his lips back to hers.

When Hunter pulled away, he couldn't help but let out a small chuckle. "I see now that you've gotten a taste of me, you don't want to stop."

"Something like that."

Hunter reached for her waist tossing her over his shoulder in a move he was now accustomed to.

"Why do you always carry me this way?"

"It's easier."

"For who?"

"Me. Plus, it gives me access to your ass." He squeezed it as he took a step toward the stairs.

"Hey!"

Hunter ignored her as he ran two steps at a time up the stairs. Sadly, for him, he didn't realize *something* else decided to take the journey with him. The moment he got to the landing and turned toward Abbie's room, Rupert walked in between his legs causing him to trip.

"Holy shit!" He scrambled through the room before losing his footing. They both ended up on the bed in a huff.

"What the hell!"

"You're fucking giant scrotum just tried to kill us."

"Don't call Rupert a giant scrotum. He doesn't like that." Abbie narrowed her eyes. To emphasize her point, the cat jumped onto the pile of clothes on the end of the bed and hissed at Hunter.

"Oh, for fuck's sake. Is this what it's going to be like dating you?"

"If by that you mean, if you make fun of my cat, I'll tackle you to the ground? Then, yes." She pursed her lips.

Well, that didn't sound bad to him.

The corner of his mouth turned up in his famous smirk. "Then I'm game. I like it when you tackle me to the ground. Better yet, I like it when you do it naked."

With that Hunter pushed some of the clothes out of his way and pinned Abbie beneath him.

# CHAPTER TWENTY-FOUR

AFTER WHAT HUNTER would describe as an interesting event, to say the least. Especially when Rupert decided his ankle was his new scratching post, Abbie fell fast asleep.

He wasn't all that surprised, after all, the plane ride was a lot for her.

He smiled to himself. So was the sex. He was doing something wrong if he didn't make her pass out of exertion afterward. And he would have been right there with her if his stomach hadn't demanded otherwise.

Quietly, he got out of the bed before donning his gym shorts. As stealth-like as he could, he tiptoed out of her room and headed toward the stairs. Once he made it to the bottom, he saw Rupert pop his head up from the arm of the couch.

However, the moment Hunter took a step toward the kitchen, Rupert meowed causing him to turn back toward him. "What do you want?"

Once he made it back to the living room Rupert popped his head up from the couch and meowed again.

"What do you want?"

He meowed a third time. "Stop doing that."

Rupert stretched in one of the creepiest displays Hunter had ever seen before he hopped off the couch and strolled over to the window.

"Let me guess, you want a treat?" Hunter rolled his eyes.

At the word treat Rupert jumped onto his hind legs pushing his paws in the air. "Fine. But just so you know, this isn't gonna be a habit." Hunter walked over and grabbed the bag of treats.

"Sit."

Rupert did.

With a creeped out shudder, Hunter tossed him a cat treat he caught in his mouth just like a dog. "When I become your dad, the first thing we're doing is getting you manly clothes, second I'm going to teach you other tricks. Maybe fetch."

Rupert hissed.

"What you don't want to play fetch?"

The cat started spinning around showing off his pink turtleneck. "I see, it's the clothes. You don't want me to buy you something with a skull on it?"

Rupert hissed again.

"You'll like it, I promise." Rupert meowed before lunging at his leg. "Oh, come on you've got to be kidding me?" Hunter tossed the treats on the floor causing Rupert to abort his mission and go after them.

"I can't believe I just had a full conversation with a naked pussy." Hunter shook his head as he walked into the kitchen in search of food. He grabbed a bottle of water before he looked through her cabinets.

Nothing.

After a few minutes of searching Hunter finally found a

bag of pretzels. They were better than starving. As he walked out of the kitchen his eyes looked to the stairs. As inviting as it sounded to crawl back into bed with Abbie, he didn't want to wake her.

So, the couch it was.

He plopped onto the sofa and started munching on his snacks. That's when Hunter saw Abbie's laptop on the corner of the coffee table. Figuring he might as well check his email, he opened it.

The first thing that popped up when the computer opened was a document. He didn't mean to, but his eyes couldn't help but scan it. His heart sank.

Abbie was putting in her two-weeks notice?

That couldn't be right. As he read the words over and over again, he decided he needed to find out more. He opened up the recent folder and saw the document titled *Checklist to start your own Advertising company:*

His eyes widened as he sat there staring at Abbie's computer.

Holy shit she wanted to start her own advertising agency.

Hunter looked back to the stairs. Why hadn't she told him?

Okay, up until two days ago she still wanted to smother him in his sleep, but now. A pang in his heart ran through him.

She didn't trust him.

He sat back on the couch in his shorts as his mind processed the new information. He wasn't really sure what to think. After looking over her checklist again, she clearly had a solid plan and was about to implement it.

Now, it made sense why she was hesitant about Robert signing the contract. She'd been planning this all along.

He took one last look toward the stairs.

Rupert jumped on the couch distracting him from his thoughts. The cat sat next to him and rubbed his head on Hunter's arm begging for attention. Reluctantly he scratched the creature. "Whoa, who knew you were this soft?"

Rupert began to purr as he stepped into Hunter's lap. "No claws there, buddy, I got nothing to protect the goods."

Rupert looked up at him with soft eyes begging for more attention.

"Fine." Hunter rolled his eyes with a sigh before he scratched under the cat's chin. "What are we going to do about your mother? She's being sneaky."

Rupert dug his claws into Hunter's thighs. "Hey, what did I just say?"

And then it hit him. Hunter knew exactly what he needed to do to prove to Abbie he was serious.

Rupert let out a small meow gaining his attention. "What do you think your mother will say when I tell her I want to go into business with her?"

Rupert purred louder.

"That's what I'm thinking." Okay, at first he was sure Abbie would throw a fit and say shit like he was trying to be the boss of her. No, he wanted to either go in as partners or he'd be her first employee.

He reached for the computer pulling open his email. He quickly opened a new message and addressed it to his old boss asking if they could meet or at least talk for a few minutes.

Hunter left on really good terms. It helped his old boss was a hopeless romantic and he pretty much pushed Hunter into going after his girl. He also promised him if he ever needed anything to give him a call.

And that was exactly what Hunter was going to do. He was going to ask advice on how to go about starting their own advertising firm.

Hunter looked back up at the stairs once again.

If Abbie was serious about this. He was one-hundred percent going to be behind her and help her succeed in every way possible.

He knew this was the thing to prove to Abbie what she really meant to him.

Abbie yawned as she finally woke up. Dang, she hadn't slept this soundly in forever.

She reached for the spot by her neck and came up empty. Her brows pulled together.

No Rupert.

Figuring he must have jumped down she stretched feeling her body ache.

That's right. A smile spread across her face.

Hunter James was in her bed.

Hunter freaking James. She never thought she'd say those words. However, as she reached for him, her hand hit a pile of clothes instead. *What the heck?*

Abbie pushed herself into the seated position and surveyed her room. Ugh, it was a disaster.

Deciding it was best to ignore it. After all, she was now a master at ignoring such things. She grabbed her robe before walking out of the room in a search for Hunter.

Not that she enjoyed waking up next to him or anything, but she... okay, she was lying, she did enjoy it. Somewhere along the line her heart won out.

At least for now.

As she got to the top of the stairs she heard a grunt followed by, "I told you no claws, you rat."

A broad smile appeared on Abbie's face.

Man, how her life had changed so drastically and so fast.

Plus, she was kind of glad Hunter was down there. With a hop in her step she hurried down the stairs.

When Hunter appeared in her line of sight her breath caught. He had Rupert on his lap and was *petting* him.

"I said no claws, dude. How many times do I have to tell you? That's my dick."

"He likes to make people suffer. It's Rupert's own brand of pleasure," Abbie announced.

Hunter snapped his head around to her. The moment Hunter's eyes locked with hers she saw a huge grin form on his face.

"Hey, baby. Did you get in a good nap? If not, march right back up there 'cause I plan on fucking your brains out the rest of the night."

Abbie rolled her eyes as her smile widened. "Do you really have to say shit like that?"

"Like what, that I want to fuck you all night? Yeah, how else are you gonna know."

"Trust me, I know." Abbie shook her head as a wicked smile appeared on Hunter's face. "Good. As long as you understand me."

Abbie walked down the remaining stairs before trotting over to him. And for the first time since Hunter walked back into her life, Abbie leaned down and kissed him on her own.

"Wow."

"Wow, what?"

"I think that's the first time you kissed me without threatening to punch me first." He smirked.

"Don't get used to it." Abbie sat down next to him. "What woke you up?"

"My stomach." He held up the bag of pretzels. "This is all you have."

"I needed to go shopping the day Bill sprung the trip on us." She shrugged. "I'm surprised I have anything."

"All you have is tea, water, and these." He plopped a pretzel into his mouth.

"The essentials," she laughed

"Sure."

They sat in silence munching on pretzels for a few minutes until Abbie spoke up. "So, this is really happening right?"

"What?" Hunter looked at her with his head cocked.

"Us." She motioned between them. "This weird thing that is whatever we are."

He leaned over kissing the top of her forehead. "Yeah." He then pulled back and cocked his brow at her. "Actually, I guess that depends."

"On what?"

"On if you plan on treating me like your plants?"

The smirk on his face made her want to punch him. "I love my plants."

"To death."

"Shut your face, asshole. Clark is still alive, isn't he?"

Hunter pointed to the plant on the coffee table. "Only 'cause your mom took care of it while we were away."

"Shut it." She picked up her plant before moving it to the other side of Hunter so he couldn't look at it.

Out of sight out of mind.

However, when Abbie turned back, Hunter was staring

at her. "I'm in this for the long haul, Abbie." He said making her heart do that stupid flip again. It was nice to hear him say it. Although, in her mind she still couldn't quite comprehend it but she liked it and the more she heard it the more she wanted it to be true.

"You keep saying that."

"It's 'cause I mean it. I meant everything I've said, Abs."

And for the first time since Hunter started using her nickname again, it didn't hurt.

She wanted to believe him. She really did, and she promised herself she was going to try.

Hunter chuckled as he nudged her shoulder. "Come on, babe. Let's go to bed." He picked up Rupert from his lap and tucked him under his arm causing Abbie's heart to melt.

"We have an early day ahead of us tomorrow.

"Why do I feel like you're up to something?"

"You're constantly suspicious."

"How can I not be around you?"

Hunter held his hand over his heart. "That hurts."

"I call them as I see them." Abbie shrugged before sending him a wicked smile.

"I'll remember this." Hunter narrowed his eyes directly at her.

"So will I."

## CHAPTER TWENTY-FIVE

Abbie took a deep breath as she held her bag tightly to her side while her and Hunter rode the elevator to the office.

Inside her purse, she had her two-weeks notice letter.

She swallowed hard. Abbie hadn't told Hunter anything about it, but she had a good reason. He might talk her out of it, and she didn't need that. This is what she wanted.

"Are you sure you want to talk to Bill first?" Hunter scoffed as he crossed his arms over his chest. "I have a thing or two to say to him as well."

"And, you can. Once I talk to him." Abbie took another deep breath desperately trying to calm herself. *You know, tell your boss he can fuck off for the stunt he pulled and then turn in your notice. Sounds like a fantastic conversation you're about to have there, Abs.*

She broke out in a sweat. *Did I put on enough deodorant?* Without Hunter noticing she did a quick sniff check. *I think I'm good. I mean, it's not like it's going to matter if I'm known as the stinky one, 'cause in two weeks, I'm gone.*

Abbie swallowed. Why hadn't she talked to Hunter

about this? *No, none of that thinking here. You are a strong independent woman.*

This was the right choice for her and once Bill knew what she wanted, she'd sit down and talk to Hunter.

Abbie had to do this on her own.

"I thought I was going to hold him down when you let him have it?" Hunter huffed with a grunt.

It was kind of cute after all. Hunter being all big and bad on her behalf, and truth be told she still wanted to punch Bill right in the mouth. His stunt was the last straw for her sealing the deal on her decision. "I'm sure it will still come to that." Abbie shook her head as her nerves started to get the better of her. Right now, this was the scariest thing she'd ever imagined.

Abbie was putting in her notice to start her own advertising firm.

What if she failed? What if she told Hunter and he laughed right in her face? What if this was the beginning of the end for her career?

Another annoyed huff came from Hunter as he leaned against the elevator wall. "I still think you should let me speak to him first."

Abbie's heart did that stupid flip as she looked at Hunter who was pouting. He really did want to tear Bill in two. A sweet smile appeared on her face. "Later, killer."

"Fine," reluctantly Hunter agreed. "But I want it noted, I don't like it."

"If it makes you feel any better. I don't either. When I graduated Bill took a chance on me. He somehow saw my potential and let me work my way up from an intern. The stunt he pulled was absolute horseshit and I want to know why. He and I need to have a heart-to-heart."

Hunter's brows quirked. "Not with your fists, right?"

With a gleam in her eye, Abbie winked at him. "Not yet."

"Okay." He pushed himself off the wall before he leaned over and kissed Abbie on the forehead. "I'll head to the break room, come and get me when you're done."

She nodded.

The moment the elevator chimed Abbie's heart jumped. *It's time.*

They both stepped out of the elevator but before Abbie could turn toward Bill's office Hunter smacked her ass.

"Hey!"

The corner of his mouth turned up in that stupid smirk. "I wanted to give you something so you don't forget about me."

"How could I?" Abbie rubbed her bottom as she sent him an evil glare.

Hunter responded with a wink. "I really wish you'd stop being difficult and let me go in there with you. It wasn't just your life he endangered, it was mine too."

She knew he had a point, but Abbie had to do this alone. She pushed up on her tiptoes before giving Hunter a kiss. "Twenty minutes. Then you can do your worst. Okay?"

Hunter looked at his watch. "Time starts now."

Abbie shook her head with a laugh as she walked toward Bill's office. A relationship with Hunter would never be dull.

Then she was there. In front of Bill's office. She swallowed hard as her adrenaline kicked in.

*It's now or never.*

Abbie opened the door.

Bill beamed at her as he sat back in his seat. "Abbie, it's

nice to see you back already. Robert's contract came across my desk yesterday. You and Hunter did magnificent work."

"I always do magnificent work, sir. I'm your best employee. Hell, I should be *your* Account Executive by now." She stepped into his office as her hands shook.

Bill sat back placing his finger on his chin. "You know, you make a good point. However, with Hunter signing on, we don't need two Account Executives."

Abbie bit into her bottom lip in anger as the words hit her. "Was that always your game plan? Bring Hunter on for the position and I'd stay where I am?"

Bill stared at her with his head slightly askew. "I hadn't really thought about it like that, but now that you've said it, yes. If Hunter is willing to join the team, the position was always his for the taking."

Abbie nodded her head as all the work she'd done for WCM flashed through her mind. "Even if Jefferson Exports wasn't a factor, Hunter would have gotten the position?"

"Yes."

Abbie reached into her bag pulling out her notice. This suddenly became easier on her part as she looked down at her words. "I have a question for you, sir."

Bill pulled forward in his chair. "Ask away, but make it quick, I've got a meeting to get to in fifteen minutes."

"I've always made it clear about my fear of flying, right? Yet you decided to send me across the country on a plane." She looked her boss square in the eyes.

"The account needed to be secured, Ms. Collins. If that meant putting aside your silly fears then, so be it."

"*Silly* fears?" Abbie fought to keep her composure. "When you booked those flights, did you even consider the Hurricane?"

Bill sat back in his chair once more. "What are you getting at here, Ms. Collins?"

"What am I getting at?" Abbie's anger peaked as she held onto her notice. "Why did you think it was a wise idea to send Hunter and me into a storm? Or, you know the fact I don't fly."

"But, you did. That's why you're my top employee, Abbie. You always do what needs to be done, even if flying is involved."

"Not into a storm!"

"You were supposed to be back before it hit. I don't know why you're getting up in arms about this? You're clearly back safe and sound. Plus, you got the contract. This is only going to help you. Now, let's put this in the past and move forward." Bill turned back to his computer effectively dismissing her.

*Oh, fuck no.*

"I'm afraid you're mistaken, *sir.*" Abbie walked to his desk and tossed the notice at him. "I will *not* put this behind me. I've given my whole career to you and you repay my loyalty with dismissing my fears. Not to mention, Mr. Jefferson didn't need the meeting right away. *You* did." Her nostrils flared. "I'm not even gonna talk about the fact you already had Hunter pinned for Account Executive, even though you knew I was gunning for the promotion. We *talked* about it. That's a dick-hole move. This whole situation is so unbelievably fucked up. I'm done. Consider this my two weeks."

Bill looked up from her letter unconcerned. "If you walk out that door, you're fired, Ms. Collins."

"You can't fire me. I'm quitting." She saw red. Who the fuck was this guy?

"To do what? Work for another firm? I'd tarnish your

name so fast, you'd be the laughing stock before you hit the ground floor." Bill crossed his arms over his chest.

Abbie's eyes widened in shock as she saw for the first time what a horrible person her boss really was.

"If you so much as tried, I'd punch you in the face," Hunter spat storming into Bill's office.

"Hunter James, nice of you to join us." Bill looked over at him.

"Fuck you. I heard what you said." Hunter stood next to Abbie who was still a little in shock at the realization of her boss. It shouldn't be that much of a surprise seeing as what he'd done in the first place, but it was still eye-opening. She'd given so much to WCM and to be treated like this was a slap in the face.

A sigh escaped Bill's mouth. "I see this is going to be an issue." He pushed back from his desk and stood.

"Of course, it's an issue. You just threatened me," Abbie snapped.

"It's business, Ms. Collins. Sometimes, you've got to play dirty. Make no mistake. I will. How do you think I got to where I am today?" He crossed his arms back over his chest before nodding to Hunter.

"What are you saying?"

"Mr. James knew all along he was getting the Account Executive position. That's what his trial contract stated."

Abbie turned to Hunter wide-eyed.

"Did he leave that part out?" Bill asked with a smirk.

*No.* Abbie shook her head. *It didn't matter. None of this mattered because I'm done.* Abbie threw her hands in the air. "It doesn't matter if he did or didn't. I'm tendering my resignation. You can try and tarnish my career all you want, but after this, there is no way in hell I'd ever work for you."

Bill shrugged. "If that's how you feel."

"You're a piece of shit," Hunter spat.

"And you're on the next flight back home I hear. I was speaking to your old boss this morning. He mentioned an email he got from you about a meeting. Sounds to me like you're headed back." Bill looked at them like he knew he'd won.

Everything froze for Abbie.

When she finally turned to Hunter, she saw the shocked look on his face.

Her heart shattered into a million pieces.

It was all the confirmation she needed.

Fuck him. As the tears pricked the back of her eyes, she fought to keep them down. Hunter didn't deserve her tears.

He didn't when they were kids, and he didn't now.

Abbie cursed herself at her stupidity as Hunter stood there with his mouth hanging open.

She knew it.

Deep down she knew it all along.

Hunter felt like the wind had been kicked out of him. How in the hell had Bill known about the email?

That didn't even make sense.

"You mother fucker!"

Abbie's words snapped him out of his shock. "It's not—"

"I fucking knew it!" Abbie pulled her fist back and punched Hunter in the jaw. "I knew I never should have trusted you. You're nothing but a lying asshole."

"Holy shit!" His hand went to his chin. She hit him. Abbie *actually* hit him.

"Fuck you, and fuck this place." Abbie turned to Bill. "Say whatever you want, but remember my ass will sue you so fast for defamation of character your head will spin." Abbie threw up both her middle fingers. "I'm out."

The moment she took the first step out of the office Hunter went after her but to his surprise, something grabbed hold of his arm. "Let her go," Bill grunted. "I'm willing to offer you a ten-thousand dollar sign-on bonus. You and I both know WCM is the best you'll ever do."

Holy fuck, this guy was out of his fucking mind. Hunter snatched his arm from Bill's grasp. "Don't touch me."

Hunter stood there in shock as he watched Bill shrug. Then a smug look appeared on his face. "When you play with the big dogs sometimes you get bit."

Fuck this, and fuck him. Without another thought Hunter punched Bill right in the nose. "Eat shit."

With that, Hunter ran out of the building in search of Abbie.

# CHAPTER TWENTY-SIX

Abbie stormed into her house.

She was pissed. Fuck that, no she was beyond pissed. When she walked into WMC that morning, she had a plan. Go to Bill's office, tell him to choke on a dick for sending her on a plane in a hurricane, put in her two-weeks notice, and then find Hunter and tell him.

Well, that all went to hell in a handbasket.

Fuck this and fuck everything.

Hunter was leaving.

She didn't want to believe it, but how could she not? He'd disappeared on her once before, why would this be any different?

He didn't even try and deny it.

Okay, well, she didn't give him much room to talk. That punch sure felt good though.

Tears formed in her eyes. How could she have been so stupid to believe him and worst of all open herself to him once again?

Last time he left he only took a piece of her heart with

him. This time he was taking the whole thing and there was no way she'd ever recover.

"Fuck him!" Her hands clenched at her sides as she fought back her pain.

Rupert came running from upstairs skidding to a stop once he saw her.

"Not now."

Rupert ignored her, meowing loudly before prancing to the treat area by the window. "Really, do you give zero shits my world is falling apart?"

Rupert meowed again. "Fine, you pain in my ass." She grabbed the bag and tossed a few treats onto the floor. "

Suddenly, Abbie's front door flung open, hitting the wall with a loud thud. "Abbie!"

The moment she saw Hunter her heart sank before her anger reared its ugly head again. "Get out!"

"No."

"Get the fuck out, Hunter. I'm not joking."

"Neither am I, Abbie." He stalked toward her with a determined look in his eyes.

When Abbie saw his angered expression, her blood boiled. *How dare he be angry with me?* "You played me, Hunter, just like you did all those years ago. I should have known better."

"I never played you. You've got everything twisted."

"I don't know how I can *twist* it. You've booked your flight and are leaving. I just wish you would have told me sooner, maybe then I wouldn't have made the worst decision in my life."

Hunter brows shot to the ceiling. "Are you kidding me?"

"I hate you." She narrowed her eyes on him as her anger skyrocketed.

"No, you don't and you never did." Abbie was flying

through the air tackling Hunter to the ground before she knew it.

"For fuck's sake!" Before Abbie could comprehend it, Hunter had her under him completely pinned. "Listen here, you insane woman. I'm not leaving. I don't ever plan on leaving."

"Why are you lying to me?"

"You're not listening." He let out a deep growl. "And you fucking *punched* me!"

"I would do it again! Let go of me and I'll kick you in the balls this time."

"Why is it so hard for you to comprehend that I'm in love with you?"

"Because you're a big, fat, egotistical, lying jerk!"

Hunter released her arms before jumping to his feet. "You are a pain in my ass, do you know that? I'm not leaving, Abbie. I'm staying right here. I saw your business plan last night and I want in. I want to be your business partner. I sent an email to my old boss asking for advice. I have no fucking clue how Bill knew about that, or why he thought I was going back. That's what the email was about."

As Abbie lied there on the floor she blinked. "What?"

"You heard me. Last night I saw your notice on your computer, then I found your plan to start your own advertising firm. I don't know, I thought I could prove to you how serious I was by contacting my old boss to ask for advice. The same boss that threatened to push me off a cliff if I didn't go after you and stop moping around. Then once I got some insight from him, I was going to do everything I could to convince you we should do this together. No one can deny we make a great team, not even *you*. My proposal is for us to go fifty-fifty and if you decided you didn't want that, I'll be your first employee."

"You found my business stuff?" Abbie jumped to her feet.

"Yes, I found it all last night. And might I add, I'm pissed at you for not telling me. What the hell, do the words I love you mean nothing to you? Why don't you trust me?"

Abbie couldn't answer him. "I can't—"

Hunter paced the room but stopped to glare at her. "Fine, we will go over this one more time since your thick head is out of its fucking mind. I love you, Abigail Collins. I am madly in love with you. I am not flying back to the east coast. I'm not leaving this state. Fuck, I'm not leaving this house. You and I are meant to be. You know it, and I know it. And it's about time you stop being a child. I don't even know why we are fighting right now."

"That's what we do!" she screamed. "We fight. We're always fighting and that's not a healthy relationship!"

"We're always fighting because you won't let your goddamn walls down and let me in. We fight because you think I'm gonna walk out on you like your dead-beat father. Newsflash, Abbie, I'm not him and will never be him. And, *you* pick fights because you can't admit to yourself, or me, that you love me just as much as I love you. And that's fucking bullshit, Abbie."

"Of course, I love you!" she yelled at the top of her lungs as tears ran down her face. "I've always loved you. I've loved you since that first fucking dare and I didn't know it. That's why when you left it devastated me! You took a part of my soul with you and I hated you for that. I hated you for all of it." Tears fell from her eyes. "I love you so much it hurts. I've been fighting it and I'm losing. I'm losing every step of the way. I hate you for making me love you."

At the weight of her confession Abbie crumbled to the floor as her sobs filled the room. Hearing herself say it out loud for the first time broke every last thing inside of her. She was never supposed to let Hunter back into her life.

She was never supposed to love him.

"Say it again."

Through her cries, Abbie managed to look at him. His gorgeous face had become a watery mess through her tears. "What, that I hate you?"

Hunter dropped to his knees in front of her cupping her face in his hands. "Say that you love me."

Abbie stared into his eyes, while she analyzed everything she could. And for the first time, she saw how sincere his words were.

There was no pity, no anger, just love staring back at her.

A small smile formed on her lips. "Why, so it can go to your big head and inflate your ego even more?" she tried to joke.

"Abbie."

"Fine," she sat back on her legs and looked him in the eyes, praying that her heart would finally heal saying the words. "I love you, Hunter. I am in love with Hunter fucking James. I loved you back then, and somewhere throughout the course of me walking into that damn board room with my tits out and you being there I've fallen so deeply in love with you it hurts. That scares me. I'm scared you're going to leave just like you did before. Just like my dad did." Tears streamed down her face as every wall she ever had up came crashing down.

"Abbie," Hunter spoke softly as his eyes pierced into her. "I dare you."

You have got to be kidding me! Right now, wasn't the time for their stupid dare off. "You dare me to what?"

"I dare you to marry me."

# EPILOGUE

## FOUR MONTHS LATER

"Stop touching it," Abbie growled at Hunter as they sorted through their documents.

"I put it there, so I'm not gonna stop touching it," Hunter said as the corner of his mouth turned up into that smirk she hated to admit she now loved.

"If you want to keep your hand intact, I would remove it from my stomach." Abbie pushed his hand away, finally succeeding.

Hunter let out a chuckle as he pulled his hand back. "When do you think you'll start to really show? I want everyone we come across to know you're spoken for."

Abbie rolled her eyes at his remark. She knew he only said it to get a rise out of her. "It doesn't matter. If you keep touching my stomach, you won't live to see it."

Hunter sat back on the couch ignoring her idle threat as he always did. "I wonder if it's gonna be a boy or girl."

"I wonder if they're going to be as annoying as you are?" she growled in his direction.

"Let's hope they don't end up with your anger issues."

Abbie put her hand over her chest as her mouth fell open. "I do *not* have anger issues!"

"You punched me in the face." Hunter eyes widened.

"Are you ever gonna let me live that down?" She quirked her brow at him. "Besides, you deserved it," she huffed out sitting back onto the couch.

"Just so you're aware, you've gotten a lot meaner since you can't have tea anymore."

Why did he have to remind her of that? Abbie missed tea and the stupid decaffeinated herbal teas did nothing for her. How was she going to survive the next billion and a half months with this alien creature inside her without her precious tea?

"Glad, I can still have some." Hunter took a sip from his mug causing Abbie to send an evil glare his way.

"Stop talking." She pointed to the document on the coffee table. "Rupert stop eating that. That's the contract with Jefferson Exports."

Hunter pushed Rupert down causing him to meow in betrayal.

"It's not my fault you're trying to make a meal out of our first account." Hunter shook the papers out. "I get it, bros before hoes, but if you eat another document, your mother will kill us both. You've seen the garden. The sunflowers we got last month didn't stand a chance."

Rupert meowed in agreement before trotting over to his princess bed in all his turquoise turtlenecked glory.

"I didn't kill them!"

"Yes, you did." Hunter sat back as he watched her with that godforsaken smirk.

"This is your fault."

Hunter cocked his brow. "Why is it always my fault?"

"It's easier that way."

"I don't agree." He leaned over, kissing Abbie on the cheek. "I saved Clark might I remind you."

"I'm gonna shove Clark up your ass if you drink another cup of tea in front of me again."

"Noted." Hunter laughed, dismissing her as he turned his attention to Rupert who as now on his back batting the air like a lunatic. "The next animal we get is gonna be a dog and *I'm* picking it out. We need normal around here."

Abbie crossed her arms. "Rupert *is* normal."

"No, Rupert is a hairless ballsack."

"He's going to bite you."

"My bad." Hunter held up his hands as he smiled. "He's a naked pussy."

She rolled her eyes. "I want a Chihuahua so I can dress it up," Abbie stated matter-of-factly.

"We're not getting a yapping dog, Abs. Besides, you'll dress up any animal we get."

"Fine, a Corgi then."

Hunter shook his head. "Oh, hell no. I already have to deal with your over the top dramatics. No fucking way are we getting one of those judgmental assholes."

"I'm gonna go to the shelter and bring home a dog." She poked his chest. "And you're going to just deal with it."

Hunter sat back with a dramatic sigh. "I'm not going to win this one am I?"

"No." Abbie moved in kissing his cheek. "And, I'm hungry."

"You're always hungry now."

"That's 'cause I'm eating for two."

Hunter beamed at her with pride which sent a warm feeling through her. "That's right you are, Abbie James."

"It's Abbie Collins-James. Get it right, bub."

Hunter rolled his eyes. "I don't know why you had to tack it on. Couldn't you've just taken my last name?"

"A Collins never surrenders. A Collins never backs down—"

"And a Collins never turns down a dare," he finished mocking her. "Yes, baby, I know. Why do you think we started this dare off to begin with?" He winked at her. "Nothing but a dare, right?"

Abbie's mouth fell open. "What are you saying?"

"With a dare, I can get you to do anything I want. You're like putty in my hands."

"No, I'm not! Take that back!" Abbie stood, lunging at Hunter pinning him to the back of the couch.

"And, I know exactly how to piss you off to get you to tackle me." Hunter smirked before he pushed his hips up into her core causing a small moan to escape her lips.

Abbie straddled his waist as she sat back. "Wait a second, did you just play me?"

"Maybe." Hunter shrugged.

"I love you." Abbie laughed as she shook her head.

"I love you, too, Abigail..." he mumbled the word 'Collins.' "*James.*"

Abbie rolled her eyes at her insane husband. "Now that our advertising business has officially launched, we have a client, Bill got his comeuppance when you're old boss found out what he'd done. Who knew he had so much pull? We're married and are about to be parents what are we gonna do next? Fly to the moon?"

Hunter sat back before rolling his hips into hers again. "I can think of a few things."

"Oh, yeah."

"But first," He kissed her. "I dare you."

Abbie's brows knitted together as she watched him. "You dare me to what?"

"Love me for the rest of our lives."

As Hunter's famous smirk appeared a warm smile spread across Abbie's face. "Done."

Thank you for reading Nothing But a Dare. I hope you enjoyed it! Was your intrigue button pushed when Abbie talked about the book she bought to read on the plane? Maybe the cat the size of a child? If so, Quinn sparks is the alter ego pen name of one Olive Quinn. Read all about Olive and Hank her best friend's older brother in Teased by Fire. Oh, and find out about the cat the size of a child too. Check out a sneak peek on the next page.

# TEASED BY FIRE SNEAK PEEK

## CHAPTER ONE

Olive Quinn glared daggers at her traitorous best friend, Miranda Parker, as the bane of her existence moved yet another piece of his furniture into her apartment. This was all Miranda's fault.

"Stop trying to murder me with your eyes, Olive." Miranda sighed in annoyance as she pushed the hair out of her face.

That only caused Olive to glare harder in her friend's direction. "I will not stop trying to murder you with my eyes," Olive whisper shouted. "It's your fault *he* is moving into *my* apartment."

"What the hell did you want me to do, Olive? I knew I couldn't leave you stranded to pay the rent on your own. You're just pissed I'm moving."

"Damn right, I'm pissed. If I were you I'd check every box you packed for surprises." Olive squinted her eyes harder in Miranda's direction trying to intimidate her.

Miranda shook her head. "How many times are we going to go through this? If I thought I had a chance of getting the job, I would have told you. I would have thought hell would've frozen over first."

"And yet here we are. Hell must be mighty cold right now."

"I'm sorry, okay. I'm freaking sorry."

At Miranda's defeated posture Olive softened. "No, I'm the one that's sorry. You've got your dream job now. I need to stop being angry and just be happy for you."

"It's a lot changing all at once."

Olive looked at Miranda, her eyes filling with tears. "I'm going to miss you. We've been stuck together since the first grade."

"Nothing's changing," Miranda tried reassuring her.

"Everything is changing. You're moving clear across the country and I only found out two days ago. I haven't had time to accept the fact my only friend is leaving me." Her eyes narrowed. "And, to top it all off, you went behind my back and gave your *brother* your room."

Miranda sighed before crossing her arms over her chest. "I don't understand why you are freaking out so much? Yeah, Hank is an ass, but if you both stay out of each other's way, you'll be fine. Plus, I've brought you the best research tool a romance writer could ever ask for. You'll be able to get a up close and personal experience on how he operates. I brought you a gift."

"If you mean the gift of an STD infested man-whore? You can keep it." Olive's eyes widened as everything clicked into place. This wasn't her best friend. There was no way in hell her best friend who she'd known for years would actually be doing this. That settles it. She'd somehow been abducted by aliens and the person standing in front of her was an imposter. *This is it. This is the zombie apocalypse we've all been waiting for*. Olive quickly grabbed Miranda's arms examining them for any sign of an implant.

Miranda snatched her hands back. "Jesus, Olive, what are you doing?"

"Checking to see if you have a tracking device somewhere," she said as a matter of fact.

Miranda rolled her eyes. "Do you ever live anywhere other than your fantasy world?"

Offended, Olive crossed her arms over her chest. "Hey, my weird brain is a masterpiece. How else do you think I come up with my stories?"

"I don't know how you function when all you think about is the zombie apocalypse or some strange alien race invading the earth."

Olive pointed at her head. "This imagination makes me money."

"How? Your brain makes zero sense. You don't even write the shit that goes on in your mind." Miranda shook her head. "Olive, you write contemporary erotic romance. Please explain to me how a brain so involved in aliens and zombies writes hardcore romance with alpha males that make all women drool?"

Olive shrugged. "I don't know. I think it's a weird yin and yang thing, you know, balance to the Force and what not."

"Fuck!" They heard from the other room as a loud bang echoed throughout the space.

Olive's eyes narrowed back at her friend as her lips thinned. "He's a big oaf, and he's gonna use his big oaf muscles to make holes in my walls."

Miranda crossed her arms over her chest. "All right, Olive, I get it. You're fucking pissed. Okay. If I were you I'd be pissed too, but there is nothing we can do about it now.

Hank is moving in. Right now, as we speak. He needed a place and you need someone that can pay half the rent. End. Of. Story."

Olive knew Miranda was right, but that didn't stop the betrayal and hurt from running through her. Within two days, everything she was accustomed to had been upended. That's a lot for anyone to take in.

"It's not like he'll be here often anyway," Miranda remarked. "He's always at the fire station, and when he's not, he'll be out with his flavor of the week."

"That isn't the point. With Hank the Tank..." Olive physically revolted. "I hate that nickname everyone calls him."

"It's stupid, I agree."

"Back to what I was saying," Olive started again after shaking the thoughts from her head. "With Hank moving in, I can't be me anymore. Olive Quinn: awkward, hates people, never goes outside or wears a bra. I'll be banished to my room or *forced* to wear a bra. I don't want to wear a bra. Bras suck and stifle my creativity. Oh god, don't even get me started on underwires. Who the hell came up with underwires for bras, anyway? I bet you it was a man. Yup, it had to have been a man. A woman wouldn't have invented something that after a little while, a hard metal wire pokes out and causes you excruciating pain; when all you want to do is walk to the store and buy some snacks. But no, instead I'm walking down the sidewalk discreetly trying to move the wire to a place where it's not trying to puncture through my skin and kill me."

Miranda chuckled. "You have a point about the bra, but you said the same thing about pants and you've grown accustomed to wearing them."

"*Not by choice!* I only wear them because you kept the

air on "cold as fuck." If I didn't wear pants these thunder thighs would have gotten frostbitten."

"I keep it cold because you have that weird obsession with the holidays."

"I do not!"

Miranda's brow rose before she pointed to the corner of Olive's bedroom. "You have a freakin' Christmas tree up."

"Yeah, what's your point?"

"It's the middle of *June*. No one needs a Christmas tree up in the middle of June."

Olive held her hand to her chest as if she'd been shot. "How can you say that?"

Miranda instantly rolled her eyes. "It's the *middle of June*. That's how I can say that."

"Haven't you heard of Christmas in July? I'm just a few weeks early."

"Christmas in July," Miranda scoffed. "Olive, you haven't taken it down in the three years we've lived here."

"Damn, Scrooge much? Sorry, my joy of the holidays makes you a bitter humbug."

Miranda held Olive's shoulders. "Please leave this apartment more often and get some fresh air. I really am worried about you."

"Do not shit all over my love of the happiest time of the year. And, stop deflecting on the fact that *you* went behind my back and moved in your brother."

"Think of all the material for your books you'll get now." Miranda swiped her hand towards the bedroom door. "His friends are delicious, what more can you ask for? Hot firemen as your personal research subjects. You can save your computer from all the viruses from those porn sites you..." She made air quotes. "...use for research."

"Hey, don't knock it. Those sites are a golden tool for my line of work."

"Whatever. It's done. Now, let's go back out there and get the rest of my stuff packed away."

Olive huffed before following her friend. "Remember those *research subjects* include your brother the next time you read one of my books." Olive couldn't help the smirk that spread across her face when Miranda's eyes widened. *Take that you, traitorous devil woman!*

"Oh shit, what have I done?"

Olive pushed Miranda's shoulder shoving her towards the door. "Serves you right."

As they walked back into the living room, Olive's heart stopped as she saw a shirtless, sweaty Hank standing in the middle of the room. How in the hell was it possible to look *that* good? He had muscles for days. Her eyes went to his abs as she started mentally counting them. Sure, half the men in her books were described like him, but that was in her mind. Men did *not* look like them in real life. And, why the hell was he looking at her like she was a tall glass of water and he was a man dying of thirst?

Her whole body shivered. She one-hundred percent stepped into an alternate universe.

"There you two are," Hank remarked. "I thought you'd left all the work to us." He nodded his head towards his station buddies that'd agreed to help move Miranda out and him in.

Olive looked around at the men scattered throughout the room. It was like a *Hot Fireman/Paramedic* calendar threw up in her apartment. Maybe this wasn't such a bad idea after all.

She turned towards her friend and smirked, which made Miranda blanch for a brief second before she spoke.

"No, we haven't left. We were just discussing something in Olive's room," Miranda announced before making her way to one of the many boxes in the living room.

"That so, and what did you and Olive Oil need to discuss?" Hank smirked in her direction.

"Do not call me that!" Olive glanced around the room for something to throw at his head. She'd grown up with Hank teasing her every chance he got, and if he thought she would just stand by and let him do it in her own home he had another thing coming.

At her annoyance, Hank chuckled. "Oh, I think living with you will be lots of fun, Olive Oil."

Olive turned back to Miranda ready to demand she make him leave when Hank yelled out, "Any of you seen Dog?"

A chorus of *no's* rang out throughout the room which made Olive roll her eyes. "Let me guess, another one of your degenerate friends?" she asked glaring at Hank.

His eyes brightened with laughter as his smile grew wider. "Miranda didn't tell you about Dog?"

Olive's eyes shot to her best friend who now busied herself with removing an invisible piece of dirt from her shirt. "No, I guess that tidbit of information escaped her," Olive sneered.

Hank disappeared out of the room leaving Olive with her brow raised and her arms crossed at his sudden departure. *Well, okay then. Clearly living with Hank was not going to be a walk in the park.*

A few minutes later she heard Hank shout, "Found her!" He then made his way back into the living room. That's when Olive spotted the largest Maine Coon cat she'd ever seen in her life cradled in Hank's arms.

"What is that?"

Hank pat the cat on its head causing the ginormous thing to tilt its face in his direction seeking out more attention, or possibly meat from a small animal being used as a sacrifice. "This is Dog," he said with a grin.

That's when she snapped. "Who the fuck names a *cat* Dog?"

Continue Hank and Olive's story In Teased by Fire.

## ALSO BY MOLLY O'HARE

**Hollywood Hopeful Series**

Hollywood Dreams

Risking It All (Danny and Lexi's Story) – *Coming soon*

**Stumbling Through Life Series**

Stumbling Into Him

Stumbling Into Forever

John & Emma's story – *Coming soon*

**Teased Series**

Teased by Fire

*Lucas & Miranda's story – Coming soon*

**Standalone Novels**

Nothing But a Dare – *This book*

**Stay up to date on New Releases**

Sign up for my newsletter by clicking the link or going to my website: MollyOHareauthor.com I also have a Reader Group on Facebook. Come hang out with me: Molly's Marvelous Clan

# ABOUT THE AUTHOR

Hey, thanks for coming to my about the author to check me out! Has anyone told you, you're beautiful and amazing lately? Just in case they haven't, I am!

So you want to know a little more about me? Well okay then. Much like any author out there, sleeping doesn't come easily to me. As it turns out, I've got horrible insomnia. Like, scary horrible. Anyway, when I was younger, to help myself fall asleep I'd tell myself stories. Each night I'd pick up where the story left off previously until it was complete. Then I started writing them down. A few months later, here I am, sharing my lack of sleep with all of you. Who said the stories in our heads can't be fun for others?

Fun Facts:

I fell out of the bed this morning. (Graceful is *not* my middle name.)

I saved a kitten from a bad accident and now it has a paralyzed arm ( you can follow my reader group for updates on Twitch).

I will call every dog I see "puppy."

Five books later and my Corgi still thinks she's the ruler of the world.

I haven't watched TV in four years.

For my 30th birthday, I held a Tarantula. (I'm terrified of spiders.)

I want to take and RV trip through the US and stop at all the State Parks.

The biggest Fun Fact... With the help of my reader group I'm trying to convince my husband to get me another Corgi.